TRUE-LIFE WALTER

Steven Romain

ISBN 13: 978-0-620-83226-7

Typeset by Amnet Systems.
Cover design by Amnet Systems.

CHAPTER ONE

Walter Sabukwana looked around his empty sixth-floor apartment before he left. The aluminium windows had preserved the stillness of the air, so the half-opened magazine pages, tissues in waste-paper baskets, and notes stuck with magnets to the fridge door remained in place. All these had forgotten the change of yesterday to today. The environment stirred a sadness within him. He could hear the ring of absolute silence in his ears and shook the thought from his head that in a minute no one would be around to hear it. He dropped his briefcase, turned, and went to open a window in the lounge. 'Otherwise it's unnatural,' he said to himself.

He was setting off to meet me, though I had no idea. His wife had gone to work and they had not been blessed with children. The building was silent as it was already nine o'clock. Thus it was that the only witness to his departure was the security guard, who waved to him as he drove away.

Walter Sabukwana knocked softly on my office door at the university and I called for him to come in. This was an unusual visit, because Walter and I were shy colleagues at the institution who conversed rarely and typically by accident.

'Walter!' I said, 'Please come in. I'm so glad it's you. Sit down, please.'

He nodded gratefully and sat down.

'I'm probably disturbing you, John,' he said. 'I apologise.'

'You're not,' I said. 'I wish I was so busy I could say that you were.'

He smiled and looked down to the carpet.

'John,' he said deliberately, still gazing down, 'I wouldn't be disturbing you if there was not a good reason. There is something I need to discuss with you if you don't mind. I know you're very kind. That's why I thought you'd give me a little bit of your time. Firstly I should tell you, it has nothing to do with work.'

'I hope not,' I said, smiling. 'Please – I'd like to hear anything and everything you'd like to say about whatever you want.'

'I knew you were kind,' he said softly, as if to himself.

'It seems,' he continued, 'that I am finding myself . . . in a difficult situation – a very difficult situation. And the truth is, I . . . just need someone to listen to me. You will not be able to help me. I can just tell you're someone who cares and might care to listen.'

'I do,' I said. This was already touching. I may be shy but Walter was something a little beyond shy. Catching his glance on occasion as he was locking up his office would seem to inflict pain upon him. He walked around the university with the lightness of the pure ideas that occupied him and moved through him. When they were troublesome and eluded his clear view, his face would be wrenched in discomfort. When they revealed their harmony, he glided over the pavements with a great silly grin that wouldn't leave. And I could see that when he was emboldening himself to engage in a conversation, even with the receptionist, he had prepared the wording of his questions beforehand.

'Well, John,' said Walter, 'the difficulty I am facing is this: that it seems I . . . may have to be divorced from my wife.'

'Oh my goodness,' I said. This was certainly unexpected.

'Yes, it's a very challenging situation.' His brow worked and the muscles of his jaws swelled. It was like watching a torrent of emotion pouring into a very fine sieve: something had to come out and it would only be the purest essence. Since he allowed himself to brood, I spoke.

'May I ask, what is the cause of this?'

'Yes,' he said, grateful for being drawn from an overwhelming emotion. When he spoke, his energy went into ensuring the correct articulation of each syllable, like the assembling of metal scaffolding. For Walter, thought was a much smoother process.

'The situation is like this. I have been living with a certain challenge for many years now. It is the challenge of anxiety. It is a severe kind of anxiety, not the kind that responds easily to medication. In fact, the doctors do not really know what its cause is. The truth is, the word 'anxiety' does not capture it. It's more like a physical feeling of burning in the brain. It makes for a powerful headache and it . . . it makes for a great feeling of . . . a tremendous sensation of . . . fear and trepidation. And the result of this, it seems, is. . .' His speech ceased. I could see tears welling out of his eyes. He sat still and wiped them away but more were welling up.

'The result of this seems to be,' he said, his voice unaffected, 'that I am very . . . harsh. The harsh feeling, which never leaves, makes *me* harsh. I am nervous, quick to anger. I am not settled, never.' He was drying his tears with his sleeves.

'My wife will not . . . it seems she will not . . . tolerate this situation anymore.'

Walter closed his eyes. I was very deeply touched by all this. The problem taking shape was real and live and was draining away all the frivolity from my mood. The trust he was placing in me was flattering. Just as I sat back in my chair resolving to be a passive presence for the moment, some thoughts ran through my mind.

'But these days there are so many medications,' I said, but I saw he was slowly shaking his head.

'No,' he said simply.

'With respect, Walter,' I said, 'I don't know how much you know about the latest drugs, but we have to investigate further. They can do amazing things – things we wouldn't dream of a few years ago.'

Sitting still with a rounded back, paying obedient attention to the pattern on the carpet, Walter answered slowly and deliberately. 'You do not understand.'

I rebuked myself and held my tongue.

'This is something else,' he continued. 'I have tried literally everything. Recently they even scanned my brain from every perspective: a very thorough examination. The doctor concluded he could do nothing for me. It was when my wife heard this that she began to cry. She gave up hope. And she told me . . . she cannot do it anymore. She is finished.'

As I have said, I found myself poignantly touched by this. What I mean is, being called on unexpectedly in this way, not to act, but only to listen, to share in the life of another, quite simply arrested me. I accepted the role I had been called on to play and only listened for the remainder of the interview. I tried my best to empathise with this poor soul who needed, more than anything, to share his life in space with another man. At the same time I attempted to encourage him to feel comfortable spending as much time as he needed to share this moment with me. He stayed a while, but only to sit hunched as he was. I was careful not to gaze at my watch or to fidget impatiently. Finally, he made the transition to normal life by rising, shaking hands, and thanking me in a dignified fashion. I had been growing rather anxious because, by then, I was ten minutes late for poetry performance.

The latter had been my pet project for some months. The idea was to initiate a live, dynamic performance of personal poetry focused on feelings about and visions of apartheid. I had foolishly undertaken the task of awakening my students to the fact that a complex of these feelings and visions existed that needed expressing, and then guiding them in expressing them soulfully but articulately. I had also foolishly booked the Council Theatre for a week of nights in November, which was now less than eight months away. My general approach to life is to take myself lightly enough that things feel spacious, but I was beginning to sense the buddings of tension within me. My students should be honing the skill of live performance and fostering the requisite confidence. At the same time they should be refining the formula of their work, but only to perform it as if for the first time, in one unique performance, or really five. The young men and women who had presented themselves to me until now had slotted into one of two categories: the category of those who spoke *as if* they were moved by some feeling enough to say something about it; and those who indeed tapped into some raw feeling but had no way of shaping it, picturing it, or singing it out to the world. For the second group there may be hope because all they lacked was a skill, but what was to be done with the first, who comprised most of the group of twenty-five? Were they a generation born without a heart? If not, where was the human desire to sing out the exquisite tragedy of a hidden life crushed and denied? The disheartening thought became nascent in me that this would be a performance of students imagining what it might be like to possess hearts. And in fact was this itself not something poetic, something worth showing?

As for Walter, my contacts with him for the next two months were not intimate. When we met about the university I saw that the scant expression of gratitude he offered came out of eyes greatly weakened. Under the excuse of the business of life, it may have been, these conferences did not become closer. I, from my side, tried to give over an expression of unobtrusive empathy, and I made sure to show that my glance followed his trail for half a minute after he left my company, in case he should turn back to check.

It is not the South African custom to call on a friend after eight o'clock in the evening. Walter, however, rang my doorbell at 9.30. When he entered I saw his grey jacket was flecked with the late-summer drizzle, as were his glasses, but of this he seemed unaware. His preoccupation set him apart and made me ask, 'Where *is* this man, because he certainly is not within those clothes?' He nodded me a greeting but did not speak and I showed him to a seat at the dining table. I offered him a tissue to wipe his glasses with but he accepted it with apparent confusion, so I indicated on which article he might apply it. The man's youthful face bore a heavy strain which seemed to shift and flow and threatened to bubble up to his skin. I dispensed with the small talk I might use to dispel awkwardness and again humbly assumed my role as listener. He collected himself in his seat, carefully wiping his glasses in the quiet room.

'John,' he said, 'I am again indebted to you for your kindness. You have a wonderful ability to offer a listening ear. And I do appreciate it tremendously.' All this he spoke with a heartbreaking logic. Under the dark pool of his facial skin, which I watched, what was the magnitude of the fire within? And however high that fire burned, the more it was belied by that unfaultable speech.

'The reason I have come here tonight, my friend, is that there has been a new development in the whole . . . the whole situation I described to you last time. And because you have a kind heart, I know you would want to know it.'

'Absolutely right I do,' I said.

'Well, John,' said Walter, 'I was contacted by Doctor Alex Tobias, who was the neurologist who performed all the tests I mentioned to you: the tests on my brain. I mentioned to you he told me nothing could be done for me. But he called me and he told me something that . . . he himself seemed very apprehensive about saying. In fact he almost changed his mind several times during the conversation. Finally he told me. He had operated on a patient in order to remove a brain tumour a year before. It was necessary to remove, not just the tumour, but also a small piece of the adjacent brain. The operation was a success, but soon after his family noticed he changed quite drastically. He was an accountant and had lived with a challenge very like mine. He had been highly nervous, agitated, etcetera, almost all the time. Now, all that had disappeared.' Walter, who had spoken these last words with unaccustomed fluency, gazed up into my eyes with such a substantial expression that I will never forget. I mirrored it to the best of my ability.

'Walter,' I said eventually, 'that's wonderful.'

'There is something else you do not yet know,' said the troubled man while he re-established his glance on the floor. 'This man: he changed completely in other ways. In essence you might say – he was like another person.'

'What do you mean, exactly?' I said.

'He became much . . . simpler,' Walter answered.

'But tell me what you mean, man!' I said.

Here he was still and silent for a minute.

'I met him, John.'

'And?' I goaded him for more.

Now he spoke with vulnerability, as if he were revealing a dream-image of intimate personal significance.

'I met him in his house. He was – is – a man of forty years, married with three children. We spoke in his garage where he was playing the drums. It was a challenge to hold the conversation because he would keep drumming as we spoke. To me he was open, kind and honest. Of accounting now he has very little possible connection. His wife spoke to me and told me he will play drums for two or three hours at a time. He will play soccer for an entire afternoon with the local kids. She said it's as if her husband vanished and a teenager took his place. This lady suffers greatly – very greatly. She is now the sole parent of four kids.'

Again came that substantial expression on his face, directly into my eyes, and I didn't know what to do with myself. I averted my gaze and cogitated. It was difficult to think.

'Walter,' I said finally, 'this decision seems to involve your wife. You agree?'

He waited a moment or two before answering with the heaviness of lead.

'Yes, it would seem so.'

He stopped there, though, for some reason so I made bold to continue.

'Have you spoken to her about it?'

Again he paused.

'No.'

'Well why on earth not?' I asked.

Several waves of strain passed over his face until there emerged, at the end, an admirable strength.

'John,' he said, 'imagine if someone gave you the choice between a status quo that is intolerable and an alternative that breaks your heart.'

I felt, of course, foolish and resolved to check my tongue.

'But,' I said 'she is certainly touched by this decision. Don't you have to ask her anyway?'

This question Walter left for the silent room to answer.

I often feel I am a very fickle person, and here I resolved to strengthen in this regard, which is why I forced silence upon myself. The raindrops had fattened and were beating on my roof. We felt as if the little thuds were the calamity we both knew was threatening my frail house.

'If you did ask her,' I said, 'and things turned out badly, she might blame herself for it. She might recall how she said it had been intolerable and then told you to do it.'

At this Walter brightened somewhat and seemed to considered the matter afresh.

Quiet reigned for some minutes.

'What do you think?' Walter croaked finally.

'I don't know,' I said. 'Can it be right to do it without even speaking to her? It's a deception. It feels wrong to me.' His gaze played over me carefully as if he were searching for some spark of inspiration.

'Are you sure you want to do it?' I asked. But this too he simply analysed with his tired eyes.

'Seriously, Walter, listen to me,' I continued. 'I don't think I would do it. If *you* are there, there has to be hope to fix, to mend, to refresh things. But what if you are simply not there? What would there be to gain if *you* would not be there to gain it? Besides, think of this,' I was now growing bold again, 'what if you went on a long trip? I mean to India or somewhere. And you would give yourself all the time you need to . . . rediscover yourself – feel like yourself again. Your wife would surely agree, if you told her why you wanted it. I'd bet you ten thousand rand you'd come back a different man.

Languidly, Walter turned his head this way and that and said, with a tone of finality, 'You'd lose.' He persisted in his benign analysis of my face, as if it, much more than my words, promised to offer something of value.

'Medicines Walter!' I screamed.

'You don't know who you are dealing with, John,' said the weary man.

The rain was starting to sound more pleasant now, like an old friend who has known you through hard times. We sat and appreciated its lively activity because our spirits were spent.

'And if you told her,' I said, 'she might say no?'

At this, Walter again brightened slightly, though he was distant from me, the object of his eyes' gaze, within the warmth of a subtle – a very subtle – consideration. Following this the raindrops beat down, on and on, singing in our ears the song of our life's predicament. 'Why?' they seemed to say. 'Because it must be.' 'Why?' 'Because it must be.'

'What do you think?' he croaked again.

'What do you mean "what do I think"?' I said. 'I think you should tell her. That's the only decent thing to do.'

He watched me.

'It would seem, though,' I said, 'that posing the question to her beforehand might lead us into certain difficulties.'

Walter pursed his lipped and nodded, and then slowly stood up. We shook hands like businessmen and he left, walking into the rain.

CHAPTER TWO

I n the university auditorium I sat on a plastic chair one Sunday morning, watching thrice-refined entries for the poetry performance, which was fixed and set for less than six months from that date. Facing me today was a tall, thinly-built young man assuming a morose attitude.

'I am dead – Where am I? – I am nowhere; I am a ghost. What am I? – Nothing but a piece of meat; I cannot speak. My lips – they took away; my tongue – they stole.'

As he spoke these words, he gestured in distaste at his body and seemed to dread glimpsing it, his face held in a posture of detestation.

'My feet – they use for their doorstops. My eyes are their jewellery.'

His voice was in fact wonderfully resonant, but this had gone on for ten minutes and it was growing more difficult for me to feign this posture of careful attentiveness to artistic merit. In order to allay my irritation and to continue to come across as collected to those assembled, I allowed my mind to stray to the unfortunate case of Walter Sabukwana. As my intellect perused the case, it settled on the subject of Jane Sabukwana, Walter's wife. I did not know her personally, as I had only seen her together with Walter at university functions. She too was an academic and she was possessed of very pale white skin. This I remembered together with the down-to-earth style about her, even when she strode in formal evening dress, as if a clock ticked off the minutes in her head, keeping her perfectly abreast of events. She knew where to be and what was next on the agenda, and how she wanted to spend the tea break, and when they should leave. Walter seemed content to conform himself to the ticking of her inner clock and followed.

This poor woman was waking up to her Sunday morning yoked not only with her known troubles, which were heavy enough, but also with a great load of which she was unaware. There was a plan afoot to annihilate her life and none said a word to her. Here I sat, perfectly aware of the state of affairs as they really were, but quite willing to leave her to meet them at whatever time they would savagely turn up. And I sat with a casualness and a coldness as if my life should remain untouched by another's distress. Besides, I said to myself, she may have said she had had enough but it has been common knowledge since the beginning of time that a woman is not to be taken at her word about love matters. Walter, who is thoroughly sensitive and raw-nerved, took one of her statements too literally and simply crumpled. It was almost a certainty she had already shed tears about the words she had said. Perhaps she was even rehearsing how she would tell him, 'I love you just the way you are, my Walter: my Wally.' And there he was, out there somewhere, planning a horror that would draw an awful shriek from the poor lady if she heard of it. How terribly out of proportion was his course of action! This was madness. The other night in my house I had been too tired and worn out to view a simple matter in clear mundane light.

I quickly gazed around the room and was appalled to see all the young men and women appraising the performance with total indifference to the live woman in question.

'No one knows me – no one knows if I'm alive or I'm dead,' intoned the lanky lad.

'I'm the dust under their feet – as they go on their way to their restaurants. I have no mouth to talk – I have no face for them to see – I am just the dust under their feet.'

Something was building up inside me. Suddenly I had risen and was stomping towards the glass doors of the auditorium. I had made my way noisily past them and in the chilly morning air I was in some kind of a state, perhaps a panic. When I reached my car, I got in and drove automatically in the direction of the building in Killarncy whcrc I kncw the Sabukwanas lived.

Although, as I have said, I am a foolish man, a childish man, my years have not been totally wasted. I sometimes claim the merit of checking myself in my tracks and considering my behaviour in terms of logical principles. Because I could clearly sense my mind wanted order and clarity, I veered off to Zoo Lake where I could take a few minutes to calm myself. Having parked, I paced around the lake, gazing at its central fountain in the morning light. I told myself as follows: there was strong reason to believe the woman was still attached to Walter, in which case it seemed compelling that she should know about the state of affairs so as to be able to halt the man before he erred. On the other hand there was the nature of Walter's report to consider. He had given over unambiguously that she felt it was over between them as it stood. Although this may have been a hasty conclusion made by a sensitive man, as we have said, it may truly be that these are her feelings. In this case, the predicament previously discussed with Walter returns to us. She may hysterically refuse to allow the procedure, or she might allow it and then forever blame herself for the consequences. Thus, if she had thrown away the present-day Walter, she must be made to feel that the consequences of the procedure do not rest on her shoulders alone. In other words, she must be made to feel that there is a fair chance for success in the operation and that Walter himself would return intact. Then, even if he did not, it could be presented that things had not turned out the way we hoped. It would be the fault of chance or the surgeon.

Based on all the above, we should present the fact of Walter's intention as if it offered some indeterminate chance of complete success. It should then be ascertained, as best we can, from her reaction whether or not she still bore an attachment to the man. If she displayed clear signs of attachment, we should reveal the bare facts that the only precedent we have for such a procedure resulted in loss of the subject's personhood. This would impel her into action. If her reaction signalled that she felt here was just as unbearable as there, we should maintain the story that the proposed intervention was risky but one in which we might throw our hopes. In this way she may see fit to agree.

'And why is it crucial she agree?' I asked myself, feeling pleased, as I turned onto the bridge. 'So there might be a chance she will take him back.' But as I treaded on, a feeling of revulsion grew within me, like the reaction we have to pettiness. Something was wrong here. Yes, why was the central hinge of all this the question of whether or not she would take him back? What about the question of what was truly right and beneficial for Walter? I recalled the unbearably pathetic expression on his face when he told me that the patient's condition completely disappeared. He wanted this for himself, not just for his marriage. That was now apparent to me. Yet this course of action was not born of a sensible mind, but one racked in chronic distress. If so, another danger presented itself, and in compelling colours. What if she had given up on Walter, was numb with the pain of a thousand painful memories, and would send him to whatever fate the surgeon wanted to risk without so much as remembering she once held him in her heart? She may feel, '*I* have nothing to lose.' After all, we are all human, especially people pushed near the limits of their endurance in marriage trials like these.

In fact, then, to revise things, it was most positively *wrong* that Walter should be left to lobotomise himself. If her devotion to him would be rekindled by the prospect of it, I could leave her to take care of the rest. If she exhibited signs of having thrown Walter away, we should in fact become Walter's defender against any of her encouragements to go ahead with the madness. Indeed, it was not out of the question that she might harbour feelings of vindictiveness against him after years of trial. This would be natural. Unless she became his energetic defender, she should be mistrusted and *we* should take up the task of protecting the dear man from harming himself.

Thus it was that a feeling of serenity settled on my bones and I directed my strides towards my car. I was proud of my prudence. The Zoo Lake fountain celebrated it. When I parked outside the Sabukwana's building, I noted the fact that I had no reason to believe Jane Sabukwana was alone in the house, as Walter may very well be there. Nonetheless, I found myself pressing the button by the name 'Sabukwana' and then wondering at my stupidity in doing so. A woman's voice answered and I said:

'Yes, good morning, is it Mrs Sabukwana?'

'Yes,' she answered sceptically.

'My name is John Legrand. I'm a colleague of your husband's and a . . . friend of his. Sorry to bother you but do you perhaps have a few minutes to speak with me? There's some . . . matter of concern to me – to do with Walter.'

She was silent but then she buzzed me in. I ascended to the sixth floor, found the door of their flat, and knocked. The lady opened the door and seemed uncomfortable in the usual sort of way for a woman alone in the house. I tried to put her at ease with extreme politeness.

'I am terribly sorry to bother you at this time,' I said. 'I hope it's not inconvenient.'

'It's a fine time,' she said. 'Please come in.' She seemed a little worn out or tired but was quite vigorous as she opened the security door and immediately relocked it behind us.

Inside the modest apartment I was gratified to see Walter didn't appear to be present. She led me through the apartment. To my left as we walked I peeked into the small kitchen where a note was stuck on the fridge with the words 'You're the best!' penned in blue ink. This brought some undetermined effect upon me. As we continued I furtively sought evidence all the while and noted several framed pictures, mostly depicting Walter and Jane together. In one, Jane had received her PhD and stood with Walter before the white pillars of University Hall. In another they leaned on a cannon at the War Museum. I was guided to a seat by a garden table on the enclosed patio. Jane Sabukwana seated herself in a dignified manner and asked me what it was I would like to talk about.

As I say, I had been affected. It was difficult to bring myself to speak at this moment because I had not expected to be emotionally clobbered by all these impressions. I was confused too. The images of the couple's smiling faces occurred before me, and it struck me how the smiles they wore were identical, though the skin colours contrasted. And those words haunted me: 'You're the best!' Was it possible Jane Sabukwana had written those words? And if so, how old could a fridge-door note really be?

'Are you alright?' the lady of the house was asking me.

'Yes,' I said, somewhat off-guard, 'fine.'

'It's just that you seemed unwell or dizzy,' she said.

'No, I'm fine,' I said.

'Well then,' she said, taking me at my word because she was rather a sturdy character, 'what can I help you with Mr Legrand?'

'I'll tell you, Mrs Sabukwana,' I said, wondering at the normality of my voice and pondering who was the conscious being who was going to bring this speech act to its end.

'I hate to pry', I said. 'I won't interfere in anything that's not my business. But your husband and I have been speaking together. We've become friends, I think. And it's just that . . . he has been saying things that have made me concerned. That's why I came: because I thought it somehow might help if you knew them. Maybe you already do.'

She clenched her brow, revealing an inner tension through her face which gave it a masculine aspect. She said nothing, though, and this encouraged me to continue.

'He has not told me anything private, I assure you. But he did mention – I think just because he felt he needed an outlet – that he has struggled for some time with an anxiety condition.'

I gazed towards the lady. A vein on her forehead swelled.

'And he also mentioned that this condition has posed great difficulties not just for him, but also for you.'

I watched her. Deeply-running waters were stirring within her. I waited some moments but then continued.

'As I say, Mrs Sabukwana, this is none of my business. The only reason I've come to speak about it with you is that Walter said certain things that I think you would want to know. There is a doctor who is offering to perform a procedure on your husband. He says there's a chance it might help Walter with his challenge but he admits it's risky. It's very risky.'

Her head bent. She sniffed and wept.

'It's not totally clear to me, but he seems set on doing it. He may have already begun making plans to have it done.'

She wept softly.

'Do you hear me, Mrs Sabukwana?' I said. 'He seems set on doing it. It's an operation on the brain. And I think he may not consult you before having it done.'

On went the poor lady's sobbing. I waited five minutes and her posture didn't change. I could only see the top of her head and a portion of her forehead, and her body shook now and again.

'Mrs Sabukwana,' I said, 'I'm not sure if you are registering what I'm saying. Do you understand me? It's risky; so risky, in fact, that the chances of success are very small. And I'll tell you what the risk is. It's that when the surgeon takes out that part of the brain, his personality will not be the same afterwards. He will be like a different person. Do you understand?'

She, for her part, could not interrupt the sobs, until finally she straightened her neck and vented her feelings through her throat in a deep groan.

'Oh!' she said, and the white pallor of her skin was blotched with red marks of discolouration. 'Do you know what it's like to feel . . . to feel you're at one with someone and then something comes along and makes you feel you have no choice but to . . . to teach yourself to be separate again?'

There I sat, embarrassed, and the chilly air came in through the open window. When I witness the free-flowing grief of a woman I feel that, not possessing the vessels for it, I am blind to half the world.

'It's like cutting off part of your body,' she said, and her speech came from the same deep place as the raw grief itself, in the way it does with women.

I leaned back and looked out the window, gathering myself. This was unexpected: she was ready to leave him to it, not out of callousness or numbness, but out of absolute helplessness. It was as he had said: as far as she was concerned, it was simply not possible to continue; to remain without him was equally intolerable. The position she found herself in was tormenting – it was one of those puzzling facts which make us feel that progress is an illusion in our lives. We progress no more than a bird does. We wake up and smell the breeze and follow it on our fatuous paths and have not the slightest concept of the greater wind patterns that are running their courses over the face of the earth. As if to confirm my deliberations, a sparrow landed upon a branch outside the window, its little head flicking this way and that, following just this scent, just these sounds, to its destiny, which would be death, but because its dance would be perfect, every flutter and every flick, and every call perfectly timed and pitched, at the end of days it will take its place in eternity. We: what kind of a dance were we inevitably to dance? The thought frightened me because I knew, whether we resist it or run with it, our feet will indeed follow that same sequence.

I gazed at the interior of the apartment. A woman's jersey was draped carelessly on a couch. There was crumpled notepaper on the carpet and the carpet smelled dusty. Dishes lay untended to in the sink. The inhabitants of this home were bent under the weight of Life. I had no right to enter this space and claim to them – these cosmic creatures favoured and guided and rebuked by Life as they valiantly strove to live and not die – how they should bear its weight. Now I heard each of Walter's words that he said in the thunderstorm more clearly. They were much more correctly thought out than my own. Who could rebuke these people for hoping? On the contrary, to grasp at life now when most people would have given up on it bespoke a bravery that tore the heart.

It seemed less than ideal for me to continue sitting in that place observing Jane Sabukwana's grief.

'I do apologise sincerely, Mrs Sabukwana,' I said. 'I did not mean to add to your grief. It just seemed to me that I had this information and that . . . I could not hold it back from you.'

I rose, repeating my apology and begging her not to see me out the house. I was gone, walking in the corridor with a hot head. Where had this woman been left now? She knew about what was to occur, but reacted with the passivity of grief. This was interesting, but often the ways of women initially seem interesting to me, until I realise it is because they are realistic. Jane was not just a smart person but was a smart woman, which doubly qualified her despair as a barometer of the situation.

She could not be blamed, and neither could I, perhaps, for clumsily trying to help. My head remained hot until the evening, when I was soothed by the simplicity of checking my postbox.

Inside was a note written in a beautiful hand with blue ink. It read as follows:

My Dear John

I felt I must inform you about the details of the procedure we spoke together about, if only out of a courtesy to you who have been kind enough to open your heart to me and my unusual challenges.

The procedure is set to be performed on Tuesday the 29th of April at 8.30 am at Milpark Hospital.

Once again, thank you for your generosity of heart and for your honest advice, since indeed this is just what I needed and nothing else.

Your friend
Walter Sabukwana

My head threatened to heat up again. The sight of his handwriting was powerfully affecting. Together with the careful diction and the sincerity, it was as if I had before me on this scrap of paper a piece of the fine stuff of the man's mind. And it was complete with signals of his personal turmoil, for it was these I spied in the quick, sharp stylising of certain letters and in an ink smear low on the page. For some reason I found the presence of the note in my house disturbing and, after noting the relevant information, disposed of it, telling myself I had no room to hoard papers.

CHAPTER THREE

Each individual has their own life before them, and each day it requires correction and attention, and simply keeping the confusion within fair limits consumes quite enough energy. I am no exception, so I might merit some small leniency when I state that the Sabukwanas drifted from the forefront of my mind for the period of a few days. When Saturday the 27th of April came around, though, it occurred to me that the 29th of the month was going to be a very important day. I became nervous but found diversions for myself on that day. On the Monday morning I drove to work severely and sat down at my desk severely and spoke with the two students who came to me severely. Something was happening and it was a very serious thing. My plan was to contact the hospital after lunch.

This I did and was eventually transferred to a sceptical surgeon who at length gave me the information that the procedure had been a success. The next morning, if all was well, he might be released. I inquired whether or not a family member was scheduled to drive him home. After a waiting period, during which an inquiry was made, I was informed that yes, the patient's wife was scheduled to meet him at the hospital and drive him home. So the couple had discussed Walter's plans openly; this relieved me. This was a time to leave a family to itself if there ever was one, so I left the Sabukwanas to themselves.

Two months passed and two months feels like a hefty period of time. I saw or heard nothing about Walter, but in my mind I often pictured scenarios that may be playing out in his home. Usually I pictured a disastrous image of implacable discord, but sometimes I imagined they might have taken a holiday together to celebrate their refreshed marital bliss. The prolonged absence of news was unbearable. Whatever result had indeed come about, the passing of each of these days must be augmenting it, and the dawn of a new life must have quite definitely struck the two fine people. By now I almost considered it as if I was not intimately connected to the matter, but had only been called upon marginally, in a small way, for a brief confidence. However, one Thursday morning when I arrived at my office, two people were waiting outside to meet me. One was Jane Sabukwana and the other was Doctor Alex Tobias, the surgeon who had operated on Walter.

They took seats in my office. Doctor Tobias' demeanour was self-assured and he began speaking on behalf of the unlikely pair.

'Good morning Professor Legrand,' he said. 'I believe we spoke on the phone briefly when you called to ask about Walter. I am Doctor Tobias. We don't want to take up your time, Professor. I'm sure you have a lot to do. So I'll tell you the reason we've come.

'I gathered from Walter that he confided in you, even before telling his wife, about his plans for the procedure. I'm glad he has a friend in all this. Otherwise he would feel terribly alone. Because he seems to feel you are a friend, we felt you were someone we had to speak to – about the situation that's come about now.'

'What's that?' said I.

'The situation we are finding ourselves in is one – how can I put it? – that is very challenging, particularly for Mrs Sabukwana because she is really the person who has to live with it. It is one, however, that I predicted, if you'll remember, because I mentioned to Walter the information about the only precedent we have for the procedure.'

'Oh dear,' I said.

'What is the situation?' continued the doctor. 'Well, I'll report to you what Mrs Sabukwana has told me about Walter's present condition. Or, would you like to tell, Mrs Sabukwana?' he asked.

She shook her head.

'Walter,' spoke the doctor, 'is not behaving like himself at all. He stays out until late at night every night with a group of youths. They go around together, playing music and drinking. His previous interests, including his academic interests, seem to have fallen away. He spends his time . . . more like those boys he hangs around with.

'Mrs Sabukwana says he is simply not like himself at all. Emotionally, I mean, he is like a different person. He is simpler and more childish. I did introduce Walter before all this to my other patient who had undergone the procedure, so he knew to expect it. You also knew, I believe. Mrs Sabukwana heard it from you. Well, it seems to have happened. Very soon after the procedure these changes became apparent.'

The man's official manner irked me, especially in conjunction with the sickening news he brought. It also bothered me that Mrs Sabukwana was content for him to act as her mouthpiece. I shot her an inquiring glance now and again but she shied away. She definitely seemed worn, and I noticed that she held one hand neatly upon the other, which lay upon her handbag. This bespoke to me that her poor spirit had been laid low in ways too thorough to imagine.

'And so, Professor Legrand,' the doctor said, calling for my attention, 'to come to the point, we thought it might help if you spoke to him. You seem to be a friend of his, someone he trusts, so he might open up to you a bit. That's a difficulty Mrs Sabukwana has mentioned: he feels threatened by her and withdraws or leaves the house much of the time. Perhaps it would help him feel rooted in his old life if a friendly figure from that life were to make himself known to him. He would have a confidante. In addition you are associated with his whole previous existence here at the university. Perhaps something might be sparked off for him: some sense of affinity or familiarity with his previous life.'

As I watched him I found it amazing how the durability of a surgeon's nature could allow for such a steady self-vindication. He had warned us, he said. And he had seemed anxious to make that statement clearly, for the books. I wanted to meet Walter now and know him as closely as I could, to derive my own impression of him. I wanted to see his eyes, hear him speak. And I wanted to ask him whether or not he regretted his decision.

'I have a question,' I said, addressing Walter's wife. 'Has there been any positive result of the procedure?'

She conferred with the doctor by means of a quick glance, as if surprised.

'I'm not sure what you mean,' said the doctor. 'If Mrs Sabukwana is facing all these challenges, what does it mean to ask if there are positive consequences?'

'I mean,' said I, and this time I leaned forward and indicated I was speaking to the lady, 'that Walter underwent this procedure intentionally and for a reason. We all know what the reason was and it was a strong reason. I understand that the risk we feared has materialised. But have the benefits Walter hoped for also materialised?'

Doctor Tobias seemed about to speak but Jane Sabukwana suddenly, in a raspy voice, said:

'Yes, his anxiety has gone. There's not a sign of it.' I and the doctor regarded her and then glanced at each other.

'Does he seem happy?' I asked.

'Yes,' she said, able to subsist in the moment in the way of those who have been beaten by disappointed hopes. From her private battles she was emerging, at least in this moment, in the form of a dignified, sweetened person. But did she spy some hope in Walter's happiness that was persuasive in some way to her mind? Or was there truly no hope? I didn't know and perhaps neither did she. So I said, simply:

'Well, that is good in itself, isn't it?'

She nodded with weary eyelids and that little spark of life still there. I promised them I would call on Walter in order to speak with him. It was established that I should come late on a Thursday afternoon, when I could leave work a little early.

I arrived at Walter's flat on a warm evening which found me in good spirits. Jane announced me to Walter.

'Walter, you have a visitor! Your old friend from the university is here!'

I looked past the lady and saw Walter seated on a couch scrutinising a magazine page. He turned away from it to look in our direction. She beckoned me to approach, so I did, and all the while he gazed at me unrecognisingly. When I reached him, he suddenly smiled a hearty smile and stood up to hug me.

'My friend!' he said. 'John Legrand, my dear friend!'

His hug was firm and heartfelt. When it was finished he decided to hug me again.

'So good to see you, my friend,' he said, sitting down and indicating I should do the same. All this time he was pleased enough to smile just at the sight of me.

'I am so glad to see *you*,' I said, telling the truth but trying to appear seamless.

'Yes,' he said through his great smile, 'I believe you *are*,' and let out a knowing laugh.

'I thought you would have come before now,' he said.

'I apologise,' I said. 'I didn't want to interfere,' and gestured with my eyes to the household.

He nodded. Mrs Sabukwana was involved in kitchen work but the clinking of dishes ceased every few seconds so the sounds of our conversation might reach her more clearly.

'I'm really glad to see you again and to see you're okay.'

'Yes,' he said gaily, 'and the good news is that the operation was successful.'

I showed him with my face I was surprised and pleased.

'I'm so glad!' I said.

He only grinned more intensely, so I pursued:

'Tell me, Walter, what exactly do you mean by that?'

He answered directly:

'I mean that I notice I feel much . . . more relaxed; I take things less . . . intensely. I feel, in general, much better. My wife doesn't seem too pleased with me, though,' he added in a low voice and chuckled.

'Why is that?' I asked.

'She seems to be bothered because I don't behave as I did before,' answered the wondrous man. Striking me all this time had been his manner of speech and the light in his countenance. He seemed, not like a child as he had been described to me, but like a more *present* version of himself. He seemed available emotionally and he spoke with his accustomed clarity and precision.

'But you feel impelled to behave as you . . . feel you must?' I asked.

'Exactly,' he said. I nodded a nod of satisfied understanding.

Mrs Sabukwana laid down a tea tray before us on the coffee table and as she placed our tea cups in front of us there was a noticeable tension between the couple. Walter's joviality became subdued until she left.

'Why don't we see you around the university?' I asked innocently.

'Ah! That stuff does *not* appeal to me anymore, John. I can tell you,' he said. I indicated interest with my brow so he continued:

'It's boring.'

'Is that so?' said I.

'Yes, definitely,' he said. I marked now that he carried more of a presence than before.

'What are you doing with yourself, then?' I asked

'Ah well! I'm still deciding on the big picture. But at the moment I'm enjoying spending time with some of my new buddies. They show me the fun places around and we have a good time. And we have a bit of a drink.'

'Very nice,' I said.

'Ya!' he said. 'You have to relax at the end of the day. This world is heavy, man. It can be heavy.'

'Absolutely true,' I said.

'You must come with us one night, John,' he said. 'You'll meet the guys and have a drink.'

There is a fiery streak deep within me that wavers between inspiration and insanity. It was this blameful object that now struck out without warning. It told me to go with him, arguing that this would be a wonderfully good method of drawing close to Walter.

'Sure,' I said. 'That sounds fine.'

Walter became excited immediately.

'Will you come tonight?' he asked.

'I think I can,' I said.

Walter began making the necessary preparations, which included some phone calls, changing clothes and deodorising. He also announced in a loud voice to his wife that he was going out with the boys together with me. I avoided her eyes skilfully at that point. Just as darkness was settling on the city, we emerged into its cool air. We sensed powerfully the freedom afforded us in the city by our healthy feet and by the facts of space and time.

I could hardly believe it as I found myself strutting along with Walter, gazing over to him and finding him at his ease, tuning a small radio he had taken out of his pocket. A steady, mesmerising beat now emanated from the little device and Walter paused for a minute to hear it before settling on it and raising the volume. He didn't seem to feel the need to speak with me but only strutted with increasing rhythm, until after a few minutes I saw his gait had become a thing of beauty, the well-executed steps of a dance performed thousands of times around Johannesburg on a daily basis. Though he never looked in my direction during the time we walked, I didn't mind not making conversation. I did not speak either and soon we strutted into a street, followed by a sub-street of that street, and a right turn into a dingy building courtyard, where a mother cat and her kittens were startled by us, up some extremely dubious stairs, where we found ourselves facing a make-shift countertop that had been declared a bar.

Presiding over it, behind the counter, was an unimpressed gentleman of thick stature. Behind him on the wall hung a hand-written menu, each item below the other in white chalk: Stout; Beer; Sweet Potion; Light My Fire. Walter exhibited a certain way of greeting the man without a sound or a gesture, but only leaned on the counter and mumbled something, which the barman found acceptable enough to reward with a capped bottle of Castle Lager. That gentleman then gazed at me with little interest but a mute question. I told him, 'Light My Fire,' with consummate noncha-lance. To my great disappointment, he smiled before turning to busy himself. The décor in the shebeen were extremely simple. In fact, there was little that was not rotting or cracked or split. There were, however, four functional barstools so we sat down. The barman called out to Walter to turn up the music, which he promptly did. I must admit that I found the experience of sitting there highly thrilling. The only thing that bothered me was the thought that my skin colour rendered me conspicuous, because here was a place where only the real locals came. My hope was that the ambient lighting would emphasise the sameness of my figure with those around me.

Walter by now had begun to dance relishingly with the insistent beat, his eyes closed and going about the business with no self-consciousness at all, like one tying his shoelace. The barman was doing the same, bopping in compact movements, perfectly in time with the beat. The assistant barman arrived and, noting the state of things, joined in with his unique style. I sat in my stool thinking how wonderful a thing it was that I was there. It was as if I were remembering now, after years of forgetting, that I was a bold, imaginative person. I was impressed with myself for approaching this real-life case with my own real-life, hands-down approach to things. It brought back memories of thirty years ago, when, for me and my friends, life was something to take your best grab at, where we walked out onto the streets at night with the same poise I had felt tonight on the streets with Walter. I found I was moving with the music, and why not? I slugged down a gulp of my Light My Fire; the burn in my throat seemed to come by both whisky and vodka and there was a mild underlying flavour of kola tonic. I slugged my glass again. The beat continued to mesmerise. After standing up to allow for more freedom of movement, I danced. As I did so, I discovered that my body sought out its own felicitous movement, and when it found that movement it sang out in health. I had not felt any sensation comparable to this one in three decades. I gulped my drink and then gulped it again to finish it off. I remembered now: I was a joyful dancer, an imaginative dancer, a natural dancer. And how strange it was to feel so familiar about myself in such an unfamiliar environment. And how doubly strange to feel comfortable engaging in the intimacy of this self-discovery in the company of these men. What a strange, unlikely thing life was.

There came a decision now, made and simultaneously agreed upon by all parties, that the dancing should cease. Walter turned down the radio and settled in his stool. His mood was cool as a cucumber, but my blood was hot and it was work to calm myself. He didn't budge his head in the slightest when he asked in a soft undertone:

'How you doing, brother?'

Struggling against my pulsing body and burning emotions, I answered:

'Very very well. Wonderfully well.'

'That's cool,' he said and he sipped and perused the room with all the self-possession in the world. Three men entered and exchanged wonderful handshakes with Walter. The largest of them then offered me his hand, and in the way of a man who does this multiple times a day, I grabbed his hand firmly in the arm-wrestle posture. This was a success, but I didn't expect the switch to hand-shake posture that followed.

The three gentlemen took shots of strong drink and promised to pay tomorrow, at which the barman was the least impressed he had been the whole evening, but he threatened them with a seriousness that was less than genuine. Walter grinned deeply at the sight of the barman chasing out his companions, after which he and I followed. Our group took the hasty departure as a good omen for an evening of good times, and we strutted with pent-up positive energy. The largest of us, whose name was Sipho haled a taxi which stopped for us. The minibus door slid open and we crammed in, but just as I was about to take the last place inside, a man removed me bodily and took the place himself. I needn't have worried, though, because Sipho immediately instructed the driver to wait. He then told the man in question that he was in fact going to be travelling in a different vehicle that evening. That man adopted a contrary position on the issue. Sipho then climbed over his fellow passengers towards the door, and as he exited dragged the man along with him out into the street. There was a tussle in the road but, despite the other gentleman's persistence, Sipho's great bulk would not be denied. Thereafter we all climbed back in and the driver began driving, until the defeated fellow popped up in front of our taxi, forcing our driver to stop. At this, several people commented disapprovingly and the driver indeed edged on, refusing to be manipulated by the ploy. The tension ended when the strong-willed fellow decided he had gained whatever he could gain from the situation, stepped out the way, and took a hard swipe at the driver's head through the window as we drove past. The force of this was mitigated by a quick duck to the left, and we were off. All the travellers immediately let out a light-hearted laugh. I stretched my neck back to thank Sipho but he didn't seem to understand what I meant, already involved as he was in relating an incident many years old to his friends.

We squeezed out of the taxi and emerged onto a grey and grimy pavement in a part of the city I had only whizzed past in transit and had never once imagined as a place of destination. We strutted on and the radio was reignited and the story of Sipho's exploits in the taxi was told, and there was a most wonderfully certain feeling that no stabler, more promising situation existed in the universe than exactly this one. We turned off the pavement into a dark building with cardboard stuck over a shattered window. Inside was another shebeen, where our entry caused an array of mildly-inquiring glances. Beers were ordered for every man, but the barman did not share the mood of the party and insisted on being paid beforehand. Sipho looked around in a most comical way, causing us all to burst into laughter. Here I remembered I had cash in my wallet, withdrew it, and handed it to the barman. This improved the general attitude towards me substantially, as I was slapped on the back and my bottle was clinked by four others when we were served.

The hilarious stories really came in rich succession now, so much so that the party was in hysterical laughter almost without a break for half an hour. I noted too, between one joke and the next, that there was no need for us to keep our voices down and found this pleasing. In fact, we imposed the sounds of our radio on the other company in the bar without batting a single eyelid. One solitary, older gentleman looked at us sourly when our beat started up, but none of us felt this need imply any change of plans. Sipho, however, did feel some reconsideration of our course had been necessitated, because he flung his bottle cap at the sour gentleman's head with reckonable pace. The cap struck its target with an audible *whack* and the party erupted in joy. The offended gentleman approached our table slowly, but before he could speak Sipho called out to him roughly:

'Yes, my friend, can we help you or can we not?'

The older gentleman was ruffled and said:

'You rough boys! You think I'm a fool!'

Sipho gave an expression as if the gentleman's heated blood were something he had expected entirely and he didn't hesitate before answering:

'No, but you deserved it, old man, so don't complain. Standing over there with your *sour* sour face. You needed a wake-up call, to remind you that you shouldn't look at nice people with a *sour* sour face like that. Don't you think he deserved it?' he asked me in particular with great expression now.

The entire party at the table looked in my direction, as did the older gentleman, who was certainly riled.

'What's that?' said I.

'Don't you agree he deserved what he got for looking at us sourly like that?' said Sipho, and the company were all silent.

'And you should know,' explained Sipho to the older gentleman, 'this man never lies. He doesn't know what it means to lie. He's so pure of heart, his skin is actually white. Look!'

The company enjoyed this, but Sipho repeated with his strong voice:

'Don't you agree he deserved what he got for looking at us with such a sour face?' The whole room was soundless.

'Um – yes,' I answered, and there was a joyous eruption on the part of all except the older man who positively fumed. Our group sensed it was an opportune time to leave, but before we did so, Sipho and another of our crowd each gave the older gentleman a great kiss on the forehead. He had evidently not been reconciled to us by the time we left though.

On we tramped, having belted another lively story to tell. All the while, Walter's demeanour was steady, downplayed and digni-fied. He spoke now and again to a companion in low tones, wearing hardy expressions of comprehension and empathy as he listened. He drank, but not overmuch. And he smoked as we tramped, in a manner which suggested it was exceedingly natural, though I was certain I had never seen him holding a cigarette in previous his-tory. He certainly was not the fellow directing our movements, but he had a way of infallibly bearing record of the group's status and intentions. Our present purpose was perpetually known, digested and accepted by him as each of his movements testified. Of course, I had made it my project to observe him as closely as I could and I pride myself on my powers of observation. I watched his gait, which I called the *camel-clip* to myself because it was the stride of a man used to crossing great distances. It was like watching someone limp with a spring in his step.

Now as we all walked, I quickened to catch up to him. After puffing his cigarette, he turned his chin faintly in my direction and said lowly:

'How you doing, brother?'

'Just fine, thanks,' I answered in a lively manner and he smiled back mildly, observing me, the tip of his cigarette glowing as he drew upon it.

'What's next on the agenda?' I asked heartily.

He hesitated before answering, seeming to assess me a second time.

'There's a concert down the road the guys want to check out. Is that okay with you?' he said.

'Absolutely,' I said. 'Do you know the band?'

'Sure I do. Everyone does. They're called Black Knights.'

'What kind of music do they play?'

'Big Beat Hip-Hop.' He gave me a smile as he said this.

We arrived at a stone building that was the centre of a hub of human movement. We walked confidently through a small courtyard where heavy bass sounds could be heard and then into the concert hall. There was a band on stage whose lead singer, wearing a tribal headdress, was pacing back and forth calling angrily for audience response. The response was unconvinced. Witnessing this for several minutes sufficed to give me an inclination for fresh air, so I left to sit in the courtyard. Seated on the clay bench in the courtyard was none other than Walter. I sat down next to him. He had been contemplating his cigarette in the dark but turned to smile at me encouragingly.

'If this is what your nights out are like,' I said, 'I don't know how you have energy for anything else.' He smiled back politely.

'Seriously, Walter,' I said, 'do you have any idea of what you plan to do in the daytime?'

'Yes,' he said, 'it could be the guys have a job for me at Builder's Project on Louis Botha as a packer. They work there and they tell me there's a place available. I'm going to try out on Monday.'

'Oh!' I said, 'and how do you feel about that?'

'Really good, man,' he said evenly.

'Do you really?' I asked.

'Yeah, sure,' he said, his right thigh relaxed over his left knee.

'Do you mean, it's hard to find a job and you're happy to have found one?' I asked.

'No, not just that,' he said. 'I like that kind of work. I'm going to enjoy it, I know.'

'Is that so?' I asked perkily.

'Definitely,' he said.

'What do you like about it?' I asked.

He gestured vaguely with his hand as if conjuring the words to describe what was.

'For me, a good day's work, when it's hard, when it's heavy carrying, is the best,' he said. 'I feel tired at the end. I can go home to sleep. Or I can go for a drink with the boys. That's all I need.'

'I can understand that,' I said. It was work for each of us to make ourselves heard to the others among the heavy bass sounds pounding in the courtyard. Walter bopped his head in tune with the beat several times.

'Must be a big change for your wife, though,' I said.

He took a breath a little deeper than usual and answered, this time with a more relaxed air.

'Ya, man, that's the whole challenge we have at the moment. She can't understand what I see in this kind of work. She thinks it's like deciding to be a beggar when you could be a prince.'

I noticed the humble spirit with which he held his hands neatly on his lap, his cigarette still burning between his fingers, and it recalled for me the fashion of his wife in holding her hands upon her handbag.

'I'm sure it's a challenge,' I said.

'Ya, man, it's not simple,' he said in a gruff voice, and the difficulty he was referring to twinkled in simple clarity in his eyes.

'Believe me, I know,' I said. 'Or at least I can try to imagine. But what do you tell her?'

'It doesn't matter,' he said. 'I tell her I feel I need to go out at the end of the day, because the day is heavy. Or I tell her it's because I feel the stress – *that* she understands better. But although she understands she also doesn't understand, because sooner or later she starts up again, asking why don't I stay at home more. Why don't I go to the university any more. Or don't I want to read a book. I wish I could do something to make her less upset.'

I attributed this heartening progress to my unusually good listening powers, which inspire confidence. And there is no question

I did want to listen to Walter, to know what was in his heart, to give him an outlet for his confused feelings. If I had found myself displaced in my own home like a stranger, through no fault of my own but only through the desire to be liberated from suffering, I too might feel at the end of the day that I needed to seek out a means of feeling like myself again.

'My friend,' I said, 'I can see your challenge is a very difficult one. I admire you for your bravery in shouldering it.'

This he took lightly, with a rhythmic bop of his torso to the music, and said:

'It's all sharp, my brother. Don't worry, because everything will be okay in the end. You'll see.'

He was a wonder to me, or at least I felt there were a few chapters of research I needed to produce before I could say I had reached some level of comprehension of this case. Tonight, being night, did not shed enough light on his face, and particular his eyes. I needed to look into his eyes, because that is how souls meet one another directly. I felt I needed to hear and see him talk to me, and then somehow I would have a clearer grasp of the case. Overall, I had the frustrating sense that the crucial cues were getting lost on me. Perhaps the Light My Fire was partially to blame, and maybe it had been a tiring week.

'Walter,' I said, 'I want to ask you a favour. And the favour is that you allow me to accompany you on your day's work on Monday, the whole day from morning till nighttime.'

'Sure brother,' he said, blowing out a mouthful of smoke.

'I just feel I . . . I'm trying to . . . come to grips with your challenge, and this might help me. I want to follow you around for the day. Besides, it will give us time to chat together. Why do we always have to have our conversations over serious matters?'

'One hundred percent agreed, brother,' he said.

'I won't get in your way,' I said. 'We've never had time to really get to know each other. Since you flattered me by opening up your life to me, I want to do my best to be a good friend. Does that make sense?'

'It definitely does,' he said, smoke drifting from his nostrils. His tough veneer, however, resisted easy interpretation. We shook hands in the blackened courtyard and agreed I would meet him at his house at 6 am on Monday morning.

CHAPTER FOUR

The sun was still a contained yellow semicircle on the horizon visible through the chilly morning air when I arrived at Walter's building. After I identified myself on the intercom, there was no response until Walter himself appeared after a lapse of five minutes. He was dressed in common blue overalls. His greeting was masculine and he turned to walk up Africa Street.

'Are we walking?' I called after him because his pace was quick.

'Ya, man. That's the only way,' he said.

'But I have my car here,' I said. 'I can drive us.'

'No, no,' he said. 'The only way is to walk.'

It was unclear to me exactly what he meant but I assayed to keep up with him. He walked now, not with the *camel-clip*, which was filled with an upbeat energy, but with the *camel-stride*. The steps were longer and the neck was held straight, rocking easily back and forth with the strides. I made a point of checking the gaits of other men to compare. Some bore similarities, but, in this place and time at least, Walter's strides seemed the most perfect.

Two kilometres passed behind us, me walking three or four strides behind Walter, and I had begun to mimic his walking style.

I found it very beneficial. As we progressed I appraised Walter a little. All that was notable was that his spare, muscular frame wore the overalls with a naturalness. There was not a trace of embarrassment about the simple blue shirt which lacked the two lower buttons, nor about the matching blue pants clinging to him by an elastic. On his feet were sockless moccasins upon which a leather tassel danced with each step. We passed a grocery store and its owner opening the security gate for the day. Walter raised his arm and cried out 'Strong!' to him. The proprietor responded smoothly with the same word. My stiff brown leather shoes were not suited to this kind of walking, but what I felt more acutely conscious of were my khaki pants and striped cotton shirt. I felt just a bit too clean and bleached to be comfortable.

Walter's path intersected with that of another gentleman of similar build, dressed identically, and who might have given Walter a run for his money by way of progress. The two greeted each other by exchanging a lively joke I could not decipher. As they conversed, neither altered his pace in the slightest, as if their legs were the turbines of a train that functioned by their own mechanism. I don't claim any universal value for my observations; I only record them in the way one who journeys to a far-off destination records his idiosyncratic impressions and thoughts. For some reason these particulars struck my sensitivities. As for Walter and the early-morning travellers on Louis Botha, these were nothing but the fabric of life. A bakkie stopped at a red robot, at which a man who had been sitting in the open back of the vehicle alighted and took the place in front that had been occupied by a lady. This lady, short and stocky, adjusted her nurse's head-covering and hustled off the road, narrowly avoiding a car. The operation was performed so swiftly and unhesitatingly, and synchronised so well with the chivalry of the man having taken the open back in favour of the lady, that again I perceived a beautiful choreography.

We arrived at Builder's Project in, speaking for myself, a state of exhaustion, ready to begin the day. After a brief inquiry, we descended the slope of the road to the left of the building that led to the storeroom. Here were bags of cement and compost as well as boards and beams of various thicknesses and lengths in a spacious area patrolled by a single man. With this man Walter interacted succinctly and then he turned around on the space with aplomb. He began lifting and moving heavy cement bags as if he had not just walked a marathon of several kilometres. I seated myself to rest my aching muscles.

Lunchtime was a relaxed affair involving white bread and sardines. We sat on some beams with our fellow workers making small talk and then some of us lay horizontally on the beams and closed our eyes. These persons were not off-put by the wake-up call of their manager but simply rubbed their faces and swung their legs around before them. When the sun's power and light was weakening upon us, the majority of us slackened in the performance of our tasks and consulted our watches. These of us communicated with those still busy lifting and then those latter also ceased from their task. The day had ended. We stalked up the tar slope to street level. Builder's Project being situated squarely on Louis Botha, that unavoidable thoroughfare, we could already see groups of people collecting near taxi stops. Some still wore work clothes but others had changed back into respectable clothes and the orange rays, hanging lethargically in the air, caressed the brims of their white hats. I felt silly about finding all this so beautiful and only gave Walter a nod of recognition. As we joined the nearest group and began to squint into the light with our peers, I noticed how some men smiled for the sheer joy of it or found some small excuse to do so.

I told Walter I was meeting him tomorrow morning again and he agreed. We parted with a firm handshake and a shy smile. He seemed to have lapsed into a mode of interacting with me on brief terms since the night out with his friends. I recalled how he had been more bright-eyed and articulate when we had spoken in his house. This was something that wanted comprehension. During the night my mind turned over images of the day in a troubled fashion. The image of the hundreds of neatly stacked beams kept returning to me. And the weatherless atmosphere of the dusty storeroom, dank and stagnant, also recurred upon my mind uneasily. In the long minutes when I tossed in my bed, new meanings kept settling upon these images, yet the images persisted in appearing after periods of break as if there was some other, truer meaning they meant to express. 'Perhaps', I thought, beginning to feel tormented, 'the beams are the explanations for the matter of Walter. One beam is the operation. Another is the effect of his fellowship with his new group of friends. A third might be that this is the Walter who always was there, finally emerging. And the stifling airless room stretching out around the beams is the over-simplicity with which we think of this matter.' There was no exhilarating sense of enlightenment, but I did feel more restful from then on.

The next morning I rang the Sabukwana's bell at exactly six o'clock and he was down and ready to go a minute or two earlier than yesterday.

'How are you?' he asked me.

'Grateful to be here,' I answered. 'What about you?'

'Sharp, sharp,' he said. 'Very sharp.' He zipped up his waist-pouch without expression and began tramping for Louis Botha. The morning was colder than the previous morning and there seemed to be less light. The shop owner on the right-hand side of the street was just arriving and identifying the key for the security gate among his bunch. Walter saw him and called out:

'Strong, man! Strong!'

The shop owner seemed not to hear and kept passing over from one key to the next, so that as we began to leave his shop behind us, Walter called back over his shoulder:

'I said: "Strong, man! Strong!"'

The fellow looked up absently and then vaguely raised his fist which bore the keys in greeting. Walter added a bounce into his step. I followed and began to enjoy the walk.

The air was cold and so dry it may as well have drifted miles over a desert before settling on these streets in the night. A group of overalled men joked loudly as they bounded in our opposite direction, and I caught wonderful expressions from their faces as they passed. Another man, walking singly, paused to light a cigarette in the cup of his hand. The wafting smoke in the stationary air and the diffident morning light was perfect. I felt a desire to smoke myself. And I felt, as I had the day before, that it was a struggle for me to fend off the power of mesmerisation inspired within me by the impressions of these streets, and to keep to my project of observation. The walk took a slightly more merciful toll on my fifty-year-old body because of yesterday's exertions, and Walter seemed not to feel it at all once again. This is despite the fact that I don't believe Walter could be more than two years my junior.

The day followed the same pattern as yesterday. Lunchtime arrived and was met with quiet relief on the parts of the workers. Twice in the afternoon, a lorry reversed down the storeroom driveway in order to be filled up with fertilizer. The driver of the second lorry, a farmer wearing a khaki button-up shirt with matching shorts, peaked his head out the window and called out to Walter that he could barely remember possessing the strength to lift bags of fertilizer like Walter could. Walter showed a hearty smile, which brought a smile to my heart, and the farmer reached out to Walter with a ten-rand note. Walter took it politely.

'Thanks Baas,' said Walter, and the farmer waved out the window and motored off. The incident touched me, yet this was not saying much since, as I have mentioned, I was oversensitive to all the impressions of these days in any case. I filed away the picture of Walter's smile in my mind. The end of the day crept in upon us and came to rest just as we felt we could do no more. Engines revved; a taxi driver pressed on his hooter; a traffic officer ordered a taxi driver to pull over to the side of the road and he humbly complied, her police vehicle's blue lights flashing in the yellow lane of the freeway, and there was just enough beauty and softness and harmony in the environment to comfort our hearts for the journey home.

I received a phone call in the evening from Doctor Tobias. He told me as follows:

'Professor Legrand, I am calling on behalf of Mrs Sabukwana. She tells me you have initiated a connection with Walter, and that you have even . . . associated yourself with his social circle, and have accompanied him to his work. We are only concerned to know where this association is going, because we imagined you would maintain a respectable distance. How is he to be reinspired with the feeling for his old life if you are entering into his world with him?'

In reply, I told him, firstly, that my approach to the matter differed from that of *we*. I was not aiming to pull some trick on Walter or cause, by experiment, some response. Walter was a human being who happened to be my friend and if *we* had any further doubts on my approach, we could keep them to ourselves. If Mrs Sabukwana wanted to communicate with me, though, she could do so directly in the future. I bade the doctor goodbye.

It was on a Saturday night – the night that carried with it an extra strain of wildness – that one of Walter's crew secured for us, somehow, the use of three motorbikes. Thus it was that, quite neatly, the six of us filed onto the three bikes. I was slotted behind Sipho and therefore could do nothing but stare into a large leather-covered back while gripping around its waist. When we started off, it seemed Sipho was learning how to operate the machine for the first time. We veered right, then left, and were forced to lay our feet down to avoid toppling onto our sides. This was while the other two bikes were speeding off comfortably. Sipho said not a word and, believing implicitly in his ability to tame this machine which weighed less than he did, kept on revving and we kept on sputtering and jolting forward until we finally eased into traffic. I sensed Sipho's urgency to catch up with the crew and disagreed with it on technical grounds, yet something prevented me from protesting.

'Where are we going?' I shouted.

He answered something unintelligible that sounded like, 'To get fresh.'

After motoring for twenty minutes we all pulled up onto the pavement outside the Johannesburg Pavilion. It was now fifteen minutes past eight, so this area was not only deserted but also bore an air of belonging to a different time of day. I felt like a criminal; my stomach thrilled with a tingle. The crew mounted the broad, low steps that families mount at midday in good weather to pay for entry to the pool. We, on the other hand, leaned on the steel railings to the right of the entry booth and beheld the large swimming pool lying undisturbed in the dark. It was a spacious rectangle, and in the dim surroundings, with the play of only a few of the street lights behind us, it seemed like a piece of the nether parts of the Atlantic, transplanted here by the cut of a great knife.

'I'm going in,' said someone named Faustus, and with that he hoisted his leg over the railings. Soon, his muscular body was dangling by his wrists and his body pasted to the wall of the Pavilion. Then he allowed himself to drop quite a distance into the dark before we heard his feet touch down, and we looked somewhat anxiously for signs of his condition.

'It's not far,' he called up. 'Come down.'

We followed. In my case, this was not a simple matter and I gave myself up for lost as I prepared to drop into the blackness. Surprisingly, I met the ground successfully and wondered why I had worried. Clothes were discarded and we immersed ourselves in the water. Our calls rang out through the stone surrounds. I may as well have been in the middle of the ocean for all I could see and feel. It was a most invigorating experience. Sipho, we noticed, had climbed the ladder to the diving board, which stood vastly above us. With a call of 'Watch out!' he was plummeting down through space for a period of four well-counted seconds. Then he struck water to sink, splashless, like a pin. His enormous voice roared up with him as he surfaced, in triumph and terror, and we all burst into raucous laughter.

We all frolicked in the moment of blind weightlessness, somersaulting and spurting water and laughing. Walter, for his part, was certainly taking part in the general spirit of things. I noted, when watching him ably tread water in the nimble way his dense muscles allowed, that even while he grinned with the broadness of abandon, he evidenced in his manner a certain aspect of cool detachment I had spied before in him. I admired this quality – perhaps it was an inner sturdiness, an unwillingness to let oneself be subject to chance. I remember wondering from where it came. In any case, Walter seemed to bear the mood of the company in pure form, as he had on our last night out. He was energetic and fearless, and had a way about him of taking projects of fun-making with the utmost, straight-on seriousness.

We didn't rush ourselves, almost as if hoping to be discovered, yet we met no response other than the echoes of our voices upon the stones. We had grown cold simultaneously, it seemed, and we emerged and clothed ourselves, shivering in the night air. I needed Walter's arm, extended from above, to hoist myself back onto street level. We started our motors, grunting and chuckling to each other in satisfaction. Off we sped again and the air was icy over our faces and down the backs of our necks.

I cannot describe the feeling that was possessing me just now, and I had never felt it before. On a motorbike, there is nothing between your skin and the tar of the road but your own clothes. And who was to know if Sipho were to run out of petrol here where he was motoring, in the most filthy, forgotten side-streets of the city? I tried to restrain myself, but when he turned speedily to the left with apparent randomness for the eighth or ninth time, I asked:

'Where are we going now?'

'Get-a-Fix,' was my answer.

We pulled up on a pavement by a building just as non-descript as the other city buildings. It was only distinguished by the presence of a capped man in drab clothes, loitering in its stairwell and eyeing all passers-by. He observed our approach, taking a special interest in me, it seemed.

'Thirty bucks,' he said.

Each set of eyes referred back to the set behind it, until mine were reached. I took this as my cue to open my wallet, after which the gentleman softened slightly in manner. Here, however, as we readied to enter, a thin youth smelling of hair-gel pushed past us, laid a note in the capped gentleman's hand, and climbed the steps without a word. Sipho showed his discontent to his comrades with nothing more than an open-faced look. This was received silently and, after our money had been accepted, we climbed the steep, narrow staircase.

As we progressed, a throbbing beat grew upon our hearing. When we had reached the second storey it was quite overwhelming and we stepped into the source of the noise, which was a dark room marked by luminous green, pink and yellow decorative butterflies. Here, various personalities lounged and smoked and drank. Others, some five or six, danced to the powerful beat in strange lame attitudes. Sipho showed how pleased he was with the appearance of things by jumping directly into an energetic dance. I was shepherded by Faustus to the bar and persuaded of the pressing need for alcohol. I could not refuse, and six tequilas were ordered and quickly dispatched. Then six more were ordered with similar results. After some dancing, we seated ourselves on pillows which lay on the floor in a ring and perused the room. Sipho's eyes were locked on the hair-gelled youth, who sat holding an unlit cigarette between his fingers, addressing a young lady animatedly.

'Watch this,' said Sipho, as he stood up to walk across the room.

'Allow me!' he bellowed, while he drew forth his lighter and struck the flame with a great demonstration. The youth was taken aback but, in his surprise, offered the tip of his cigarette to the large man approaching him. Just as he began to hold the flame steady before the youth, Sipho turned the gas dial of the lighter and a gigantic flame poofed up from his hands, singeing the youth's nose. The boy grabbed his face and fell to the floor, rolling. Our crew took this hilariously. Walter, sitting inconspicuously and smoking, couldn't suppress a smoky giggle.

'What's the problem?' asked Sipho, returning to us. 'Some people just don't appreciate when you try to do them a favour.'

The degree of attention the youth herewith received suggested it might be discreet to leave, so we trooped down the steps back to the cold night. We bid the capped doorman a casual farewell and mounted our bikes. The general hilarity allowed for some flexibility in our usual cautiousness about rules of the road, so we rode all three bikes abreast of each other and Sipho managed to lift the front wheel of our bike off the road for a terrifying moment. It was as we coasted along upon the streets that had been left to our disposal that a white vehicle approached us at speed from the rear. Its roof began to sparkle with blue lights and a siren sounded briefly but loudly. We slowed and pulled over to the side of the road.

A substantial white man exited the police car and approached us with a slow watchful gait. He demanded to see our licenses. Unfortunately there seemed to be some irregularity in the documents we produced. So it was that he belligerently ordered us to follow him back to the police station at a close distance and threatened us that if that distance widened, the results would be dire.

The police station at this time of night was cold and dingy and was lit by dull yellow light. The only man present in the main room was a single officer on duty behind the reception counter, reading a magazine. We were told to seat ourselves on the benches before the counter. Walter, Faustus and I lined a single bench and, as we did so, the police officer on duty took notice of us, standing himself up unhurriedly. He appraised us with a distant air, and then our compatriots on the other bench. Sipho, facing us, leaned toward us and told us he was glad for the opportunity to complain about the quarrelsome character in Get-a-Fix. Walter chuckled. At this, the attending police officer shouted out stridently.

'What are you laughing at?'

Walter gazed up at the officer, who was thickly set around the neck and gut.

'I said, what are you laughing at?' he demanded.

Walter only watched him as he stood there behind the counter.

'Are you deaf?' bellowed the officer. 'I'm talking to *you* – yes, *you.*'

'Me?' said Walter.

'So you *can* speak!' said the officer. 'Yes, I want to know what you were laughing at. Is something funny about what's going on?'

'No, sir,' Walter answered lowly.

'I can't hear you!' bellowed the officer.

'No, sir,' answered Walter.

'I know what you are,' said the officer. 'You're one of those guys who think life's a big joke. Everything's a big joke. Nothing's serious. You're already not a young boy, I can see, but still you behave like a kid. Everything's a joke! Isn't that right?'

Walter shifted uneasily. I felt the need to protest.

'Excuse me,' I said, 'but he wasn't laughing at you.'

'I didn't ask *you!*' yelled the officer. He circled around the counter, approached us, and stood over Walter.

'What happened to your tongue?' he demanded. 'You were just laughing and laughing with your friends. The popular boy! Now you've lost your tongue.'

'I think you misunderstand,' I said.

'Quiet!' he yelled to me frightfully.

'I think the popular boy – the fun-loving boy – is learning a lesson tonight! – that he's not such a big boy as he thinks.'

Walter fidgeted and murmured, 'Sir?'

'I hope he doesn't forget his lesson too quickly, so he won't need to get another one!' exclaimed the officer.

Walter held his head steady now, facing ahead and slightly bent, his eyes down. The walls of the place cruelly repeated the officer's merciless tone, adding a shrillness to it. I felt I should defend my friend but this officer had left the bounds of self-control. We all recognised the painful position we were in and sat avoiding each other's glances.

The officer who had brought us in was waiting tactfully for his peer to finish his tirade. Now he walked up through the centre of the room and lay a clipboard on the reception counter, filling it in as if barely noticing the situation behind him. The awful gentleman standing over Walter glared at him in unabated ferociousness. I wished more than anything that I could save Walter the effect of that glare because he seemed to suffer so because of it. He had ceased wincing and flinching completely and only sat dead still, facing ahead as if bound by ropes.

As it happened, the officers on duty were unwilling or unable to lay any serious charge against us. They tried to fill us with the fear of the law and only a fool would have spoken up even for a moment to detract from their sense of dominance. We sat and listened as they told us the seriousness of our crime and that from then on we would carry with us a criminal record. We watched as they tarried and filled out forms dramatically and tarried again, and after two hours we were released with a stern warning to drive straight home and never be seen again riding our bikes without a license.

On Monday morning Walter was different. He didn't call out a greeting to the grocer on our way to work. He slunk instead of bounding. He barely spoke to me and seemed to carry a great weight silently on his shoulders. In addition I thought I spied something new in his manner at certain moments – sarcasm. When he met the floor manager at Builder's Project he received his instructions wordlessly and sulkily. He looked up at the manager with eyes troubled by an enforced passivity. He moved from one task to the next, and then into the lunch break, as if being forced against his will to go through the movements. His whole being declared he did not want to be questioned, though, so I did not approach.

On the Thursday evening of that week we walked all the way home because there was a taxi strike. Being mid-winter, the sun was well and truly down by the time we had reached the mid-point of our journey and the streets were in shadow, the horizon emptied of all but some pale red light which showed behind our backs. Walter walked some fifteen steps ahead with small relentless steps. At a point somewhere past halfway he veered off the island upon which we were walking to cross to the pavement on our left, which was cast in darker shadow. He slowed, hesitated, by a parked car, and I heard the smash of a pane of glass. Then again I heard the sound of a smash. I approached Walter curiously and found myself wonderingly witnessing him break into the car. He was reaching through the broken window to open the car door, and when he had done so he applied himself to the radio with a screwdriver for a minute before emerging with it, whole, in his hands. He tucked it under his jacket and walked along smartly. I said nothing and followed.

When we were arriving at Walter's block of flats, I saw he was about to turn to enter so I called to him:

'Walter! What are you doing?'

He slowed himself and turned around to me rolling his eyes, like a child being reprimanded.

'Why did you do that?' I asked.

'What do you mean?' he said under his breath.

'You robbed that car!' I said. 'Why did you do that?'

Now here was a fact that puzzled me maddeningly, namely that he became as lucid as can be, as if simply changing gears.

'Just what do you know about growing up on the streets?' he asked me sharply.

'Nothing, I assure you,' I said. 'But did *you* grow up on the streets?'

'In a manner of speaking, yes,' he said.

'How is that?' I asked.

'My mother was always struggling to keep us out of the gutter. The threat of being thrown out on the streets always hung over our heads. She may have managed to keep us out, but that world has always been my world. Besides, you don't know the neighbourhoods we lived in in her difficult times. Do you think all that just disappears for someone?'

'I don't understand,' I said. 'You've never done anything like this before, have you?'

'You really don't understand,' he said. 'Maybe I have, maybe I haven't. It doesn't matter. If you had lived through what I've lived through, you'd know how things like this are just normal for me. They're bread and butter.'

'But what need do you have to steal? Are you that badly off?' I asked.

'Every little bit helps. Put it that way,' he said. With that he unlocked the front gate with his key, nodded hello to the security guard, and plodded towards the elevator with the radio under his jacket.

Two weeks later, as my mind was readying to retire itself for the night, I answered the phone and was met with the voice of Doctor Tobias.

'Yes, Professor Legrand,' he said. 'I know you might not want to talk to me but my concern is for Mrs Sabukwana at this point. The situation is just becoming untenable. Walter is deteriorating day to day. This is what Mrs Sabukwana tells me.'

'Would you please explain what you mean,' I said.

'Yes,' he said. 'Walter's behaviour has become suspicious. Mrs Sabukwana tells me that all through the night he is visited by all kinds of people, who come and go nonstop. She doesn't know what to think other than that he has begun dealing in illegal drugs. It's simply intolerable for her. She's in a state of terror. He himself barely talks to her. For her, it's like having a strange and threatening stranger in the house all the time. Well, not all the time, because he's only there at very late hours.'

'He doesn't give any explanation at all?' I asked.

'No,' said the doctor, 'and he's become unpleasant and almost threatening to Jane. He's sullen and silent and speaks to her very gruffly. This upsets her terribly. He has taken up the spare room and doesn't allow her to enter. It's totally untenable.'

'Untenable, I see,' I said. 'Tell me, why do I keep on receiving phone calls from you, Doctor Tobias? Why isn't she the one phoning me?'

'I've taken an interest in helping the poor lady,' he said, his voice rising in pitch and volume. 'I really take exception to your hostility. A man takes of his own time to see to the needs of a pathetic woman who has no one in the world to help her, and he's spoken to in this way! It's hard to understand. Are you not concerned about her? Do you realise what she's going through? Besides, I wouldn't be in contact with you at all if it weren't that you had taken it upon yourself to know him personally. I need to speak to you because there isn't anyone else who might have inside knowledge on the issue. But if you have nothing to say, that's fine. That in itself is helpful. We know, then, we'll have to deal with the situation as we see it.'

'Wait,' I said, 'I do know inside information about Walter. Of course I do; I've been spending hours of my time with him in the past weeks. How could I not?'

'Well, that's exactly why I called,' he said, 'to find out what that is.'

'Walter – it's become clear to me – is a complex character. The effect of the procedure – I sometimes feel I'm close to pinpointing. It's not simple. You see, he wasn't this way from the beginning. He is affected by things in subtle ways I'm trying to understand. But – certainly I've seen much room for hope – much room. In some ways he seems improved – actually improved. He has been more personable, for example. I feel that with a bit more time, his . . . condition will become clearer and we'll be able to help him settle down.'

'Professor, with respect,' he said, 'your feelings are less important than the concrete facts you can report. What does it matter to know the subtle ways he is affected? Will that make Mrs Sabukwana's life easier? The fact that he is so volatile is not cause for hope; it's cause for more concern.'

'No, no, you misunderstand me,' I said. 'I meant I've seen very promising signs I need to investigate. With regard to his present behaviour, I'm going to confront him directly and get to the bottom of it very soon. We'll be in contact, alright?'

'Alright,' he said and hung up. I did not know what he meant by 'deal with the situation as we see it', but I disliked it because it seemed to imply resorting to official channels in some way.

I tied my scarf tighter around my neck as I neared the building. It was twelve thirty at night on a Tuesday and winter was having its say in the form of the cold night air. The day had been sunny. I watched my steps as I walked, certain phrases of my conversation with Doctor Tobias playing over in my mind, but I tried to shake them away. There was a whole way of thinking in his speech that I wanted to shake off. I told myself: when dealing with a person, you can stand outside the circle and try to pull them out, or you can walk inside with them, and then walk out with them. I wanted rather to do *that*. I disliked not only the steely way of thinking, but also the dark threat of invoking officialdom. I didn't care, I told myself, that none knew of the subtlety of the thread I was attempting to find and grasp. I wouldn't care if there was not even a language to express my hope. Somehow, a fine and particular path was set out for me to tread myself, and this path spelled out the word 'hope' for Walter. You could deny it, certainly, and call me a dreamer a thousand times over, but for some reason I felt strongly compelled to believe.

I arrived at the security gate outside Walter's building. A single brick held the gate open, so I entered. The security guard, who had been dozing, widened his eyes at me and nodded. On my to the elevator I was overtaken by a large man smelling of cologne, with a thick, shaven neck and head. He greeted me with curt edginess and we waited for the elevator together in an atmosphere less than comfortable. We entered and he immediately turned and pressed the number six, thereafter asking me what number I wanted. I told him the same. We arrived with a ding and the gentleman pushed off ahead of me. I made my way down the corridor and saw the large fellow was headed directly and purposefully to the same destination as me. The kitchen door of Walter's flat had a separate entrance, and it was this one which invited entry now by means of the gaping security gate and the door left deliberately open. The thick-necked man hesitated slightly to give a soft knock on the door but then entered directly. I followed on his heels. Inside was a busy, smoky scene. Four or five men were standing around the room, each contributing the scent of his choice cologne to the small room, as well as the fumes of their cigarette. Each stood with an air of impatience, which seemed to lend energy to the way they smoked.

My stocky companion took his place at the rear of the loose queue, standing as if restraining himself with great difficulty from pushing ahead. Now I saw Walter stroll casually into the centre of the room. He walked barefoot wearing faded black jeans and on his torso both a white T-shirt too small by a size and a loose navy bath gown. He was in a very good mood. He conducted himself on easy, friendly terms with all his visitors. Just now his gaze couldn't but settle on the six-foot-four gentleman before me whose head shone by the naked globe hanging in the kitchen.

'I don't know you,' Walter addressed the gentleman. 'Who told you about me?'

'Danny – he's my buddy,' he answered.

'Danny – who's that? – oh you mean that blond kid?' said Walter.

'Ya,' said the large man, grinning uneasily. 'That's the one.'

'I barely know him,' said Walter dismissively. The large man ceased grinning.

'How do I know you're cool?' asked Walter.

'I'm cool. Trust me, I'm cool,' he said.

'Are you *cool* cool?' asked Walter.

'Yes,' he said. '*Cool* cool cool.'

'You'd better be. It's very important to be cool,' said Walter. 'I'll attend to you in a minute, after I finish with these people.'

At this, the man's fearsome shoulders seemed to rest a bit more easily. He had till now eclipsed me from Walter's view.

Walter bade someone a cheery farewell and, when he shook his hand, Walter deftly passed into it a plastic bag that was most certainly not empty.

'Take care of yourself, my friend,' Walter told him warmly. 'You have to take care of your body in winter.'

This man left with a great smile, and three similar handshakes quickly followed with the other visitors. Then the thick fellow, whose turn had come, spoke something with particularity into Walter's ear, upon which Walter nodded and receded into a nook in the kitchen where the washing machine and dryer stood. He emerged about a minute later and nonchalantly reached out a hand to the gentleman, who passed some paper money into it. At this he glanced briefly, and then he said good-naturedly:

'Good doing business, brother. Come back any time,' and Walter graced the gentleman with his very own special handshake.

This pleased and relieved the large fellow palpably. He effused a generous smile and made a respectful departure.

When Walter saw me, the cheer drained from his eye.

'You're not pleased to see me?' I asked. 'I thought we were friends.'

He demurred, circling the room in a mopey fashion. He seated himself heavily in an office chair which rolled back on its wheels, buried his hands in the pockets of his bath gown, and looked up at my face.

'You have nothing to be suspicious of,' I said. 'I have not come to reprimand you or give you any kind of talking-to.'

He turned his head at an angle, appraising me carefully from his comfortable vantage point.

'So why have you come?' he said finally.

'Because not too long ago you showed up at my house and reached out for help to me. I am very glad that you did because now I have a real friendship where before I didn't.'

He lowered his eyes, rocking his body in a slow nod and swinging from side to side on the office-chair. Then he checked my sincerity with a sudden glance.

'Have a seat,' he said. I did. He kept on silently swinging from side to side, averting his gaze. My eyes wandered to find a red glass hookah pipe standing on the floor.

'Can we have a smoke?' I asked, pointing to the pipe. He hesitated, seeming to check me again.

'Sure, we can,' he said, and he bent to clear out the pipe of its used tobacco. He refilled it, using practiced fingers, covered the tobacco with a fresh piece of foil, and then took a safety pin and delicately poked several holes in the foil. He clasped a small flat coal in a tiny pair of tongs and lit it with a match. It burned with sparks until it was scorching hot all the way through. After placing it upon the foil, he pulled on the mouth of the pipe several times until the water at the base of the chamber bubbled vigorously and thick clouds of smoke came through into his mouth. Then he handed me the pipe. I tried my best to imitate his technique.

'Inhale from here,' he instructed me, pointing at his solar plexus, 'not here,' pointing at his throat. This I attempted with some success. The water in the chamber bubbled away and filled with smoke which was drawn steadily into my pipe, and I was surprised to feel it didn't burn at all but entered my mouth, nose and lungs very smoothly.

'It's chocolate flavour – the tobacco,' he told me. 'Can you taste?'

'I believe I can,' I said.

'But it has some other things mixed in with it,' he said.

'Is that so?' I said. 'What would that be?'

'Hash and magic mushrooms,' said Walter.

'Is that so?' I said.

He nodded with a somewhat diabolical expression and released an enormous puff of smoke through his nostrils.

There was unmistakably a change that overcame me in the moments that followed. I felt that the vista of a lifetime's journey was contained in the contours of Walter's face, and that the short curls of his facial hair was the forest from which I was emerging. The sunset was somewhere just beyond my view over his head, where I felt I was just on the verge of finding it. The scene around me was speaking in the most vivid of language, or languages, and it was all I could do to hold my attention upon it. Unexpectedly though, Walter spoke from the face that was his, as if that face were not so many other things.

'Are you alright?' he was saying. I tried to ascertain his real meaning. It was not easy. I decided I would take him at face value.

'Well, thank you,' I said.

'Good,' said Walter, but he changed from being a forest to being a wolf as he said it. I took this casually.

'Another puff?' offered Walter.

'I'd better not,' I said, 'I seem to have forgotten who I am.'

He smiled, puffed out some smoke, and lay down the pipe.

'Come,' said Walter, 'let me take you for a tour of my house. I don't think you've properly seen it.' It seemed like a wonderful idea, so I followed him out the kitchen, but on the way I was caught by something. A message – a blessed message – had been placed by Providence right in the sight of my eyes, because Providence knew I was a seeker; a seeker for my true path in life. 'You're the best', Providence had penned for me in a most thoughtful note and stuck it on the fridge for me to see. This was the kind of moment that affirms one on one's path in life and gives one the strength to go on.

'You know,' I said tearily, 'I really appreciate this. Thank you.'

Walter, peering over my shoulder now, asked, 'What is it?'

'Do you see the thoughtfulness?' I said, gesturing at the note. He could, and we walked through into the main body of the apartment. Walter was leading me through the lounge, which was a luxurious, soft wonderland. He allowed himself to drop onto a leather couch. I was too stimulated by the array of visual opportunity for anything like that. There was a painting of the scene of an African marketplace from a high vantage point, a tiny brown figure walking down the street between the stalls. All that could be recognised of him were three or four of his dreadlocks, which pointed into the air. Other than that, the only thing one could say of him was that he was postured in mid-step. I was struck by his smallness, in relation to his environs, and told him:

'You must be accustomed to long walks, my friend.'

But then I was not satisfied.

'You know what,' I said, 'I want to know who you really are.'

And in that moment, which was an unremarkable moment, because this fellow was simply on his way back from purchasing some nails at the marketplace on a hot afternoon, the shapes of his bunched hair emphasising the shapes of the palm branches behind him, he looked up at me and smiled a smile full of humour. In fact he may have been laughing there to himself, no one to know him in the place surrounding him, contextualising him, but finding hilarity in the fact that I knew him. The wrinkles of laughter could be detected somehow among the shade on his face. And it occurred to me with a start that he may have been laughing at me. Unpleasant, though, as this was to perceive, it was in fact clear to the eye. He was laughing that the only colours I had to see him in were the few colours painted on this canvas, and the only shapes I had to see him in were these few crude strokes in black, and yet I had the audacity to feel as if I knew him. I felt insulted.

'Let me tell you something,' I said, 'for someone whose face is white and grows up seeing white faces, to see a brown face is like seeing a different kind of thing. I know what you think: you think I view you like part of the scenery, like a palm tree – a peculiar kind of palm tree that walks. Well I'm *trying* to do better. Can you ask more?'

He simmered down a bit after that, but he was still giggling, that's for sure.

'What's that you're saying?' asked Walter.

'Me?' I said. 'Nothing. There's just someone here who feels himself superior to the rest of the human race.'

The back of Walter's head was facing me so I circled around to seat myself facing him. I could see from the cloudy expression in his eyes that he too was feeling the effects of the magic mushrooms. He smiled kindly at me. At this I was intensely embarrassed and lowered my eyes. I noticed on the coffee table there was a large picture book about Charlie Chaplin.

'Charlie Chaplin!' I said.

'I'm a big fan of his,' said Walter.

'Really,' I said. 'I would never have thought.'

'I've seen all his films hundreds of times,' said Walter. 'When I was a kid, I used to get back from school and just watch Charlie for hours.'

'I don't think I've seen a single one from beginning to end,' I said.

'Oh, you must,' he said dreamily. 'Charlie is the best.' Now he grew pleasantly involved. 'The thing about Charlie was that he was Everyman. He just used the humanity in his face and he got our hearts; no words.'

'No words, I like that,' I said, but I wondered at the relationship between Charlie Chaplin and Walter because it was so unexpected. Then, as my mind was dispersed in wrestling with this fact, as well as with the intensity of all my impressions, something happened which captured all of me in one go. Walter was miming, Chaplin-style, in the dead silence and dimmed lighting of the lounge. At first I felt extremely awkward by it and wished it to stop, but I giggled to show my support and encouraged myself to simply be present and absorb the performance for however long it should last. Walter took to his feet and the length of the lounge had become a freeway, because he continually looked up and down it, expecting a bus. He kept on referring to his watch worriedly, sometimes close to fed up. Then he began hitchhiking with a look of bare hope and 'please!' One car whizzed past, and another. I felt wondrous things I could never put into words, and I literally was clinging to the arms of my chair. Among those things was an intense empathy for the man. The rainwater on the street was wetting his shoes and pants; he was pitifully attempting to erect his umbrella but in vain. I could not help however because he was in a different world: a silent world. I could do nothing but follow his fate with the eyes of my soul. I could not escape either or look elsewhere because his performance spoke so engagingly the language of the soul.

Now he had been spun around by the rush of a passing car, had fallen to his knees, and was soaked to the bone. I was reduced to struggling amorphous material within. He raised himself with great fortitude and shook off his umbrella. He squeezed out his hat. His eyes looked down the freeway sadly, then up it with doubled sadness, as if he weren't bitter but simply sad that the street's plans hadn't coincided with his own. He took his folded umbrella and began humbly tramping up the street. Suddenly a note of ecstatic hope flashed in his face. He followed a car with his eyes as it slowed to halt. All the disappointment vanished from his features like a cloud and was replaced by hearty gratitude. He told the driver a hundred thank yous as he approached the vehicle. His hand was extended in brotherly greeting to the driver when he froze in that posture and flinched his face down defensively, then again to the left, and again to the right. Some things were being thrown at him: tomatoes, eggs. He pursed his lips with great dignity, removed his hat and shook it off, then smeared his face clean with his sleeve. He dusted off his jacket slowly and methodically. His face showed he had been tried by this last experience and had had about enough for the day but not quite enough that he was world-weary. He smoothed down his tie and replaced his hat. A resolve to persist crystallised in his face, simple and questionless.

Onward he tramped, and with a slight limp this time. My soul moved with him as he made his way onward in the rain, his umbrella having refused to open again. He gazed around the busy world with a humility of a schoolboy; here passed a tram, there a taxi. Now, however, his eyes had caught something which held some promise, perhaps. In fact, a potent sense of relief now permeated his whole countenance and his entire body. This was wonderful. In what form had his salvation come? Though his eyes had first been squinted into the distance, they now focused on – me. He waved at me in joyous relief. I checked behind me and found no one. His joy grew with the passing of the seconds. Now he was beckoning me to him. I giggled. He continued to beckon; his joy was unreserved, like a relative after a long separation. There was such earnest pleading in his face I found I was compelled to stand up and meet his call. This I did with a terrific thrill. Each step I took towards him had a thousand doubts attached to it. His arms were spread broadly – I was trotting over universes. Finally we met, and I entered into his embrace. What was this hug? I thought, as it continued on, while Walter squeezed me warmly. Was it real or part of the play? I separated myself from his grasp enough to glimpse his face: it expressed mimic rapture. He was still completely in character. I recommitted myself to the embrace. What did it matter – real or fake? It was real, because right now these were the conditions under which it could happen. It was real: through and beyond all the details surrounding us. All of them had disappeared in the magic of the brotherly embrace. That was my reality and it did not matter to know his reality.

I was hugging – a drug-dealer. I was hugging – a thief. I was hugging – a professor. I was hugging – a friend. Something had changed within me: some reservation, some separation that had long been a part of me was melting away. The tears welled up and I didn't keep them down. There were so many things I wished to say. I wanted to say, 'I'm sorry'. I wanted to say, 'I love you.' I wanted to say, 'I fear you.' But instead I said nothing and hugged Walter; for an eternity I hugged him. And he hugged me back, with no reservation either. Only, through the corner of my eye I noticed Jane Sabukwana watching us and then withdraw into the corridor leading to the bedrooms.

The magic of the mushrooms diminished with the passing of another hour and I gathered my used self, which felt like an old sponge, and made my way out into the still night. I was forced to pull over twice on the way home in order to weep, but at some point discovered I had parked in my parking space at home.

Within four days I found I was contacted by a Mr Mark Sinnesan, social worker working for the Ububele Family Centre. He spoke to me very politely and told me I was invited to come to the centre to discuss with him the case of a Mr Walter Sabukwana which had been referred to him. The meeting was set and I arrived at three o'clock on the following Monday afternoon. The politeness continued now and I was ushered through a multi-coloured waiting room into a conference room where Mark Sinnesan stood to shake my hand, and where Jane Sabukwana sat demurely before the table. I greeted the lady and sat myself down opposite her, Sinnesan to my left at the head of the rectangular table.

'Professor Legrand,' started Sinnesan, 'I understand you have very kindly taken it upon yourself to assume the role of companion for Walter, Mrs Sabukwana's husband. And from what I understand he certainly needs a companion at this time, so firstly I'd like to commend you for that. He's lucky to have a friend like you.

'I'll tell you why we've asked you to meet with us this afternoon. We've been in communication with a Doctor Alex Tobias, the doctor who performed Walter's procedure, who also has taken a close interest in the case. He expressed to us his concerns regarding the changes Walter has been experiencing, some expected and some unexpected. For example, we know about some of the personality changes that Mrs Sabukwana has been struggling with. And may I take this opportunity to commend Mrs Sabukwana for enduring what very few wives have to endure, and very bravely.' Mrs Sabukwana blinked some mascara onto her cheek but otherwise made no movement.

'Most recently,' continued Sinnesan, 'we have been told about the unusual night conferences that Walter has initiated in the kitchen of their home. From what we've heard there seem to be signs that Walter may have started selling illegal drugs. I'm sure you can understand Doctor Tobias felt he could no longer keep silent and was compelled to seek assistance, both for Walter's sake and Mrs Sabukwana's. The situation is, from what it appears to him, unbearable at the moment.

'My job, Professor, is to establish whether patients like Walter are capable of continuing a normal life or should be transferred to facilities that are suited to care for them. We have a facility in Benoni that is geared to assist patients of Walter's kind. But in making our assessment we obviously need to make use of all the information at our disposal. We want to ask you if you can confirm or deny any of the impressions Mrs Sabukwana and Doctor Gur have had of Walter, because it seems you are more intimate with Walter even than his wife at this time. And for the sake of honesty I'll tell you, Professor, your relationship with him has become so close, Doctor Tobias has expressed his suspicions whether we should trust your reports as objective. He has already expressed his opinion clearly that Walter should be taken into the care of a facility.

'Well, let me start with this question, Professor: is it true, as far as you know, that Walter has begun dealing in illegal drugs?'

I felt the sense of a considerable weight upon my chest, as if it were the burden of my crime. I felt the two sets of eyes which were set upon me as if they were much more.

'Drugs?' I said. 'I have no knowledge that Walter has been dealing in drugs.'

'It's not true,' burst out Mrs Sabukwana. 'Then what are the endless late-night meetings?' She was in tears.

'Just a minute, Mrs Sabukwana,' said Sinnesan. 'We need to give the professor the opportunity to speak. Please, go ahead, Professor.'

'As far as I could ascertain, the people who gather in the Sabukwana's kitchen come for social purposes. They're a group of lively youngsters who seem to have taken a liking to Walter.'

'Then why the endless coming and going?' Jane asked fiercely.

'I have no idea,' I said placidly. 'These kids have the habit of constantly moving. They visit this friend, and then that friend, and then they go out to a bar. That's the way they spend a night out these days. I'm also from a different generation, Mrs Sabukwana.'

'I don't believe it for a second,' she barked and turned away sulkily.

Sinnesan was rather more pleased with what I had said. He smiled encouragingly.

'Yes, I know what you mean, Professor. And you would know, being that you spend your days with them.' I admitted the point.

'But Professor,' continued Sinnesan, 'have you noticed any kind of criminal behaviour on the part of Walter, or any dangerous or threatening behaviour at all?'

'No,' I said. 'You must understand. He conducts himself with a lot of liveliness, almost like a kid at times. He knows how to enjoy himself. But I've never seen him do anything really dangerous or criminal. Even his liveliness is not all the time. At work he behaves very stably, like any other worker.'

'Is that so?' said Sinnesan, penning on his pad.

'What do you mean "stably"?' asked Mrs Sabukwana. 'He's totally unpredictable. He's a different person from one day to the next.'

'That's where I disagree,' I said. 'After the procedure he was very volatile, it's true, but it seems to me as time goes by he's steadying out.'

'On what basis?' she asked sharply.

'It's hard to explain. It's something difficult to pinpoint,' I said. 'It seems to me there are reasons for each new turn in his behaviour. There's an inner thread to follow which explains his changes and his trends.'

I wondered not just at hearing myself openly lie, but at the very definite act of defense that I was performing. Had I lost the track of my sanity? Was I tampering with a delicate family matter in a careless, wanton spirit? What was really motivating me? Perhaps the voice of Doctor Tobias was really the voice of sanity in all this story. I felt my knees weaken.

'May I say at this point,' said Sinnesan, 'that it is not altogether clear what you mean, Professor. Mrs Sabukwana needs to know, coming out of this meeting, if there is any reason for hope that she had not been aware of until now. You seem to be telling us that there is, but what exactly is that reason?'

My spirit was a turmoil of activity, which seemed to be the activity of rallying to defend against an attack. I took a moment.

'What I mean is the following,' I said. 'Walter was thrown suddenly into a situation that I don't envy and in which I don't believe any one of us would be confident of succeeding. He has had to reacquaint himself with himself as if for the first time. And in addition there has been no one who could either explain to him what he is going through, or even lend an understanding ear to him in his struggle. He was left completely alone. As the friendship between us has grown, though, I believe some of the weight of his circumstance has been relieved from him.'

Take note that here again I found myself about to lie in a bald-faced way.

'I have noticed that in proportion to the intimacy of our friendship there has been a stabilisation in his conduct. Just the other day he freely embraced me. That's not just a sign he trusts me. It also shows he is learning to channel his emotions in a healthy way. Am I not correct?'

'You very well could be,' admitted Sinnesan as he penned.

'Well, Mrs Sabukwana, what do you say to that?' asked Sinnesan.

She was applying a tissue to her cheeks with infinite weariness.

'I don't know,' she said. 'What can I say? To me, it's all just words – worthless words. What do I see? One day is worse than the next. Each day brings some new unexpected insanity.'

She dropped her forehead on her wrist like a great weight.

'Didn't you see him embrace me?' I asked her.

She brooded, staring at the tabletop.

'Yes,' she said heavily.

Sinnesan's eyebrows arched up.

'Well, I see we have perhaps established there is some room to expect progress,' said Sinnesan. 'Now, Professor, I'm going to have to be in contact with you more frequently, to see if things really will develop as we hope, but I feel confident letting things continue as they have been as long as you are still resolved to develop your friendship with Walter. We'll have to meet again in three months. Mrs Sabukwana, does that sound like a fair arrangement to you?'

The lady, it seemed, could not feel her life more burdensome.

'It sounds to me like a crazy arrangement,' she said. 'Neither of you appreciate that I'm the one who is actually forced to live with the man. I married him; I've spent most of my life living with him; I'm able to see all that's good in him, believe me. But you're both talking in a dream. He's gone. The man I married is not there anymore. I can see that. And if your heads were screwed on straight you could see it too.'

Two, then three teardrops splatted on the tabletop. I was disheartened by that fact that I agreed with her precisely.

'Mrs Sabukwana,' began Sinnesan cautiously, 'listen to me for a second. I have experience in these things. I definitely don't know everything, but one thing I've seen first-hand is that there's no telling what a relationship can do for a man. I know it must be painful that that relationship is not with you, for whatever reason. But maybe we should celebrate the fact there is any relationship at all Walter feels open to.'

She only shook her head, shedding tears, in the sphere of her private emotional climate.

'And I am not proposing to let things go on forever. All I'm proposing is that we give this a period of time and see what happens. You have my phone number. I'm available to you. If it comes to it, I'm willing to go through all the necessary measures. But these are not measures we go through lightly. So I agree with Professor Legrand for the moment that we should wait and see.'

'I think you've both lost your minds,' she said.

Sinnesan looked at me. I showed him a very subtle look of indulgence, though I would have wagered half my wealth she was correct. Thus it was that by sheer manipulation, the meeting resolved to my advantage. As far as I was concerned there was no discernable reason why I had even done it. If I had not, the meeting might have resulted in a fruitful resolution to take this situation in hand. The dimensions of the situation were completely beyond me, which fact sickened me all the more at my incomprehensible bravado.

I went for a night walk in Illovo because my muscles felt an itch. Results were needed; but what was a result? This was like trying to figure out the chemical formula to heal a ghost. As I paced, a moment of inspiration was coming upon me. In a week's time would be the annual PhD Club Bash, the occasion on which the PhD students met in my house for the purpose of keeping up social bonds. The atmosphere was traditionally very light and the air full of humour. Indeed I looked forward to it in general. I pictured Walter and Jane Sabukwana arriving at the bash and something seemed felicitous in the image. Somehow it might be that the light atmosphere would work well upon Walter, would break an association of constraint he associated with the university. In addition, the formality of going out to an event together might be a welcome relief for the couple. Perhaps Mrs Sabukwana would feel aired-out by traveling with her husband into a public space, and by feeling like one of the normal couples in the room taking a night out. Furthermore, I would be bringing the field of my observation into my own turf. I would be more at ease and able to speak on my terms with Walter, and he would be captured apart from his peers.

I telephoned the Sabukwana residence and Jane answered. I told her as follows:

'Mrs Sabukwana, now listen please, there is an idea I have had which I strongly suggest you go along with. Come with Walter to my annual students' party in a week's time. It will be a light way of reintroducing Walter into the university setting. Plus, it will affirm the bonds I'm trying to build with him, and I'll tell you the real reason it's a good idea: let him feel for a night he's a part of a couple and not a youngster out on the town.' Jane Sabukwana pondered silently for some moments but she had been convinced. The only question she asked me was:

'But what if he refuses to come?'

'Then tell him,' I said, 'he can leave at any time if he doesn't find it's his scene. Tell him I only want to spend some time with him relaxing and drinking beer. Also, the students who will be there have no acquaintance with him so there will be no awkward meetings or awkward questions. Tell him, if you need to, I've come to value our friendship and I desire to maintain it.' She paused but then agreed and the phone call had ended.

It was on a Sunday night that my students started to arrive at my house for the PhD Bash. I had decorated my dining room with streamers and balloons and crammed the table with cold beers, vodka, coke, chips and biscuits. Just before nine o'clock, ten out of the twelve of us had arrived and were conversing gaily in groups about Kipling and Joyce, or Virginia Woolf, or the French Symbolists. Then it was that the Sabukwanas arrived, impressing me tremendously with their entrance. They tread softly in the room. I met them with a walloping welcome that was much over-done, but Jane smiled in shy gratitude and Walter shook my hand firmly. They moved along to introduce themselves to a pair of students standing near the couch, exchanging whispered phrases with each other as they went. Walter wore a leather jacket and carried himself in a subdued manner.

After forty-five minutes of free socialising, I initiated the traditional game of the PhD Bash. It went in this way: I called upon all people to assemble near the dining table and produced before them an old brown coat belonging to myself. Then I explained the rules:

'Now listen, all, the rules will only be stated once and any rebellious personality who dares not to listen will be punished severely. Each of you lovely individuals will be assigned an identity. You must then stand up before us and argue why you are exactly the one, and no other, who should be awarded this wonderful, this grand and honourable garment. Is that clear? I hope so, because I won't repeat a word of it. Now listen, you, Dean, you are Joseph Stalin. And you, Ross, you're going to have to be Jan Smuts because you've become such good friends with him lately. Alexa, you are Karl

Marx. Oh, Mrs Sabukwana, you are a sheep. And you, Walter, I'll tell you who you are: you are a millionaire oil merchant. Now let's go, no shirking or procrastinating. That won't be tolerated. Dean, you're up, let's go Mr Stalin.'

Dean argued that the reason he was the most fitting candidate for the prize was that, if he did not win it, he would kill all the other candidates. This received generous applause. So it was that we continued, the beer and vodka loosening our minds and our tongues, until Mrs Sabukwana's turn came. She took the coat in her hands, caressed it gently, and assumed a most pathetic voice.

'Oh, do please give me this coat,' she begged. 'I do so need it. I am only a poor cold sheep who must graze in the fields in the coldest of weather. Who will take care of me if you don't? My shepherd is a cruel, cruel man. He sheers me and shaves me and leaves me bald. And then he leads me out into the chilly rain and says, "Now graze!"'

Prince, a student, called out, 'How cruel! Terrible!'

Jane Sabukwana was mimicking a sheepish expression and this won her much favour. She continued:

'So if you don't take mercy on me, no one will, and I fear I will catch cold and die. Don't you have enough mercy in your hearts for an innocent sheep who never hurt anyone?'

The response was riotous and my heart was swelling with joy. Two or three of the men called out that the sheep had won their vote.

Now Walter accepted the coat from his wife who sat down modestly and a little embarrassed. The room quietened. He took the moment to appraise the coat in his hands. My nerves had been drowned in beer so I gazed in simple curiosity to see what would occur now. At that point Walter started speaking thoughtfully.

'You know,' he said, 'I don't need this coat. This coat is nothing to me. I'm a . . . I'm a multi-millionaire. My wardrobe is full of the best, the finest coats and jackets money can buy. Don't you guys know that?' He uttered these words with such smoothness that there were two or three outbursts of laughter.

'Yeah, we know that!' called out Prince. 'So why should we give it to you, man?'

'I'll tell you why, man,' said Walter. 'I'll tell you exactly why. But I don't know if your . . . mind . . . is open enough to realise. I need to know that your mind is open and your ears are really listening before I can tell you. Because there's no point in telling somebody something when their ears are not open to hear.'

'Tell us!' shouted Prince. 'Our ears are *so* open.'

'I don't think they are yet, my brother,' said Walter, infusing the whole crowd with a shock of excitement so they bubbled with mirth. 'Because you've all been listening to the arguments of the sheep, of Karl Marx and Jan Smuts, and when your ears hear their arguments you nod your heads and you smile and you say, "That's a good argument". But what you don't see, my brothers, is that all their arguments are all nothing. They are *no thing.*'

A little riot broke out.

'Karl Marx is nothing!' called out one of us.

'Yes, nothing,' continued Walter. 'And when you listen to *my* words, you'll know what a real argument is, but only if you open your ears and your minds before you listen!'

'Tell us, man!' someone yelled.

'Here they come,' said Walter. 'My words are coming. Are you ready for my words? Listen closely and open your ears. Here they are: I need this coat . . . to remind me . . . of where I came from.'

Prince was enjoying this enormously.

'Oh my goodness!' called Prince, catching his breath. 'Did you hear that? Did you hear what he said?'

'I can see *that* man's ears are open,' said Walter. 'Now listen again: if I don't get this coat, do you know what a dangerous man I will be? I will . . . rampage and . . . treat all my workers terribly. But if you give me this coat, I'll remember I'm really very small.

I'll remember I won't live forever. And all my workers will be saved from my . . . *terrible* treatment.' He ended with this flourish and dramatically flung the coat before him onto the couch. Prince started the standing ovation and most of us followed. Right then and there the coat was awarded to Walter.

This had been a heartening experience for me in ways difficult to explain. I felt how wondrous it was that my inner thoughts – those which had occurred to me that night on the streets of Illovo – had materialized in such concrete results. Jane Sabukwana's heart had been lightened; she had glowed with relief. What precisely we had witnessed in my lounge on that night was not clear: what this partial or total artificiality? How was he wielding his will during the performance and why had he innervated himself to do what he had done?

Following this came a crashing challenge, though it was a time I greatly craved relief. I answered my ringing phone one Wednesday evening and I found it was Jane Sabukwana on the line in tears. The trouble was that Doctor Tobias had performed a follow-up brain scan on Walter and had given them a prognosis which was decidedly bleak. He had stated that based on the abnormal brain activity detectable on their most modern of machines, Walter was and would remain abnormal for life. The chances of recovery of normal brain activity were about five percent. Very much contrary to the doctor's hopes, he was sorry to say, the regeneration he had been expecting to see in the scan was not present. What had Walter's behaviour been like in the interim? Jane answered with reports of the daily and nightly behaviour well known to me, and Doctor Tobias stated that this should be reconciled with his prognosis. This is what he would have expected to occur, based on the new results. He did not mean to be conveyor of bad news, but he felt he should report what facts lay before him. What was more, Jane reported to me, Walter had reacted to the report by fleeing wordlessly. She had no idea where he had gone or what his intentions were now. She felt a terrible sense of foreboding. What should she do?

I told her not to worry. I believed with absolute firmness he would be discovered soon and I was going to do my best to hasten the discovery. She should do nothing at all and leave it to me. I would contact her very soon with good news. Regarding the medical prognosis, I told her, I had nothing to say at the moment other than this: that I was not completely convinced by it and that I believed time should be allowed to run its course, and that there was no doctor nor any machine that was infallible. Had we not seen the revival of our hopes on the night of the bash, I asked her?

'I told Doctor Tobias about that,' she said, 'and he said it didn't imply any reason for hope.' The doctor hadn't been surprised by it at all. Walter had only grasped the rules of a game and played the game. The adult behaviour, the integration of self, the sensitivity to social norms, all these things were affected by the deficiency in brain activity and these would not change. I told her again that I hesitated to say anything drastic on this point but my heart told me to keep hope alive. This she accepted with a pitiful act of will and it was with this very gossamer note of hope that I replaced the receiver on its stand.

I found, when I inquired with Builder's Project, that Walter had disappeared without an explanatory word. Thus it was that I took to cruising in my car up and down Louis Botha Avenue at various times of day but particularly during the morning traffic to work and the evening procession back home. I had some fancy that among this dynamic throng of life, if I searched thoroughly enough, he must be found. Of course it made no sense, but I persisted anyway and with an odd sense of confidence that inevitably I would indeed find him. But I would tell myself as I made my way home with the coming of night that I was pursuing nothing but my own fancy, since I had become so infatuated with that street.

On a Friday afternoon I was enjoying the hot dry winter sun penetrating the windscreen of my car and warming my shoulders as I drove up Louis Botha towards Balfour Park. Builders spoke one with the other in subdued conference on their way to their taxis. Shop assistants pulled down the aluminium security gates. The road workers continued their work. A tractor driver casually mounted a red mound of earth which seemed too steep to be mounted, conversing all the while with one of his peers, and an orange-suited lady stood in the weakening light waving a red flag to the motorists. On the pavement several workers lay prostrate, resting, by an open hole in the ground. My eye caught the countenance of one of them, his eyes shut in a moment of peaceful escape. It was Walter! I struggled with all my will to change into the left lane, take the first left, and park in the first available spot. I rushed back down the street, doubting myself severely as I continued on my way. There was the figure lying on the ground. I approached carefully, and when I reached him he was sunk in too deep a slumber to notice.

'Excuse me, sir!' I said. There was no response. I repeated myself in a louder voice. The man lay stationary and I called myself a genuine fool for standing here bothering this innocent person.

'I'm very sorry, sir,' I called, desperate, 'but could you please look here for a moment!'

He rolled over onto his back and looked into my eyes. The face was sooty and sleepy – but it was Walter!

'Walter!' I said. 'Don't you know how worried we all are about you?'

He appraised me spaciously, half dreaming and grinning ever so slightly.

'Good afternoon, John,' he said. 'You seem nervous. What are you so nervous about?'

'You just disappeared!' I said. 'We were worried about you.'

He didn't hurry to give an answer, but turned his face towards the sun to bask. The sun's final call, at this hour, was so clear and pure that his brown skin seemed like pure gold. His smile broadened, his eyes closed, and he murmured:

'I really do not know what you are making a fuss about. Jane's life is relieved by my leaving. When I am there it troubles her so much. Why would she want me back?'

'Why would she want you back?' I said. 'Because you are her husband and she loves you. That's why.' He only kept on basking. Then his dreamy murmur started again.

'And I don't understand what you want of me. What do you want of me?'

'Nothing,' I said. 'I don't want anything of you.'

'Yes you do,' said Walter. 'You want me to be something – I don't know what. What does it matter to you what kind of life I lead?'

Among all the sensations that were upon me, especially the heat of the sun and the interminable progress of the cars, it was difficult to register what he said. I chose not to give a snap answer, but waited. I thought perhaps he had fallen asleep again but after a minute and a half, he spoke.

'And if you are thinking of my wife, you know that she will be totally fine after a short time.' He rolled over onto his left shoulder again, showing me his back.

I knew only that there was no answer to this in my heated brain, nor was there one in the scene of the lumbering, clumsy bakkies and vans rolling on patiently in traffic, nor in the tired faces of their drivers which didn't even budge to gaze at me. Now he may really have gone back to sleep.

'Well,' I said, 'let me ask you a question: are you happy with the way things are?'

He rolled onto his back again and gazed serenely into my eyes.

'Yes,' he said.

His manner was supremely difficult for me to decipher. Either that, or it was as simple as simple can be.

'All this dirt,' I said. 'These streets. Walking miles and miles. No money. What about your health?'

This seemed to give him pleasure. His smile actually showed teeth now.

'Is it not lovely?' he said. 'Why would you think it is not? I don't understand you.' He rolled over onto his side again.

'But I want to tell you something important,' I told him. 'What the doctor said: that is nonsense. It's not true. He examined the results again and changed his mind. The report means nothing. It means nothing, Walter, do you hear me?'

His sides inflated and deflated with a gentle rhythm.

'It means nothing to me too,' he said.

'I don't think you really understand,' I said. 'The report he gave you is actually rubbish. It's a mistake. I don't think you're really listening to what I say.' These last words were uttered so desperately that he stopped and took note, half rolling back towards me.

'But it really makes no difference to me,' he said, 'whether his report is true or false. Let it be true! And let it be false again! What difference does that make to me, my friend? Now listen, don't answer me, John, but listen to one question I have for you. Look up in the air,' and he pointed up.

'That bunch of dandelion from the little bush on the side of the road – do you see it? It's floating up on that wind and separating in the air. One little spore will float up over Kew and might end up landing in someone's garden over there. Another little spore will miss that wind and get caught up in another wind going up Louis Botha and then fall on someone's windshield and be wiped off with the car's wipers. Another spore will just hover in the air over here for an hour and then come down to rest on some lady's hat and she'll take it home with her. But look at them now, all still hanging together in the air, John, and answer me: isn't it true that where one of them will go, that's the place for him and no one else?'

He had such a way of speaking that I was arrested by him. It reminded me of a performance I might have once seen. Yet on the other hand, what could be less theatrical than what I was witnessing? One thing about which I felt a certainty was my feeling that it was wrong and futile to argue with him.

'Yes,' I said, 'it is true, Walter.' And the engines of a series of trucks deadened the space between us of all sound. While I waited for the vehicles to pass, Walter curled up in a foetal position on his side and waved me away with a hand that was hugging his shoulder.

CHAPTER FIVE

I made sure to contact Mrs Sabukwana as soon as possible and inform her Walter was in good health and living in the vicinity. She need not worry for I had initiated contact with him and he responded very freely. Also, he was as lucid as I have ever seen him. This was true, strictly speaking. The only question in my mind regarded the material of whose lucidity we were speaking. But this question I kept to myself. My message for the lady was to try to be patient and leave it to me and hold fast to hope.

I was not going to lose the subtle thread of progress that I felt was within my grasp. At five o'clock in the afternoon I drove to the same site on the freeway where I had found Walter working the previous day. This time I found him hacking into the tar with a pickaxe, drawing the heavy tool over his shoulders to swing it down again with perfect rhythm. The work was not light but his lean body didn't rest. He noted my presence when I had been standing by him for several minutes, and it was only with a glance that darted momentarily up from his work. He said nothing.

'Let every dandelion spore go its own way!' I called to him. He could afford only to tarry for another short moment to glance at me before lifting up the iron tool again.

'Let each go his own way!' I said. 'I agree with you. I have thought about it and now I agree with you.' He chopped on and on, intermittently shooting up his gaze to me.

'But can't two dandelion spores meet each other and know each other along the way?' I asked, and here he planted the great tool at his side and panted heavily as he watched me speak.

'*Don't* be something for me, for your wife, or whoever. Fly your way. But since we've met, let's remain friends. Why do we have to fly away from each other and pretend we never met? Why do we have to become part of the furniture, part of the background for the other one of us?'

He nodded very slightly, looking into my eyes, as he stood there catching his breath and leaning on the pickaxe.

'I have something to ask of you,' I said, 'if you agree with what I'm saying. I'm going to Cape Town because I have to visit the university there. Come with me for the trip. We leave on Monday.'

He leaned for the moment on his thighs to catch his breath more quickly. Then he stood straight and crinkled his brow as if to say, 'What's the use?'

'This is important, Walter,' I said. 'Wherever you go from here on, there will always be someone who knew you. I won't judge you against someone else's measurements. You need that. And so do I.'

His chest was heaving less vigorously. He gave me one last appraisal with those steady eyes and then nodded.

'I'll do it,' he said.

I reported to Mrs Sabukwana there had been a great victory. This is exactly what was needed, I argued to her over the phone. Walter should be isolated from influences old and new. All the environments and people, carrying the powerful associations they do, should be distanced. I was convinced wonders would come from this trip. It happened, thankfully, that I inspired trust in Walter and was thus in a position to bring this experiment into being. Jane acquiesced, not finding herself in a position to do much less.

During the plane trip, Walter's mood was very agreeable. He smiled very readily in sheer excitement at the journey. He would show me magazine pictures that amused him. The gentleman seated to his left asked him the time and Walter entered into a congenial conversation with him about that gentleman's grandchildren. He chewed gum and, when we landed, looked out the window the whole time it took the plane to land and come to a halt. I was content to speak about the stimuli in our environment. We were two friends on a recreational trip together and nothing more.

In what followed next I could perceive, for all that I had been left to feel alone and helpless, that it was only for the Great Designer to draw me close in the end and show me how near at hand my poor life is to His great interest. My purpose in travelling to Cape Town was to visit a small reading room in Hout Bay, not little known but unknown. It is maintained by a private collector by the name of Howard Graves and is named after one of the rare volumes it houses: *My Rudyard Kipling*. On the old wooden shelves of this small room, whose floors creak volubly, are several uncommon volumes on the famous author's life. There are twenty-one handwritten documents from the pen of the great man as well as a handful of sketches and paintings depicting him grandly. Several of his possessions are also on display including a game of Jacks said to have been his own as a child, a fountain pen, and an atlas with notes in the margins.

There was one particular diamond I sought in that unpopular room, which I am certain does not hear the sound of more than a couple of footsteps in six months. It was a volume written by a man named Adrian Einhorn, the name of which had become the name of the library itself. In this thin volume, which no one would dream of publishing more than once, Mr Einhorn had devoted himself in the second chapter to describing his eight-year-old impressions of Kipling personally telling a story to his class in primary school. I had seen a single obscure reference to the book and what had drawn me to journey all this way to the Cape was the description given in that reference of Einhorn's project. The author had written the following in a footnote at the bottom of the page:

> See *My Rudyard Kipling* by Adrian Einhorn where Einhorn conveys his own experience of Kipling's performance as if it touched the innermost, most refined apparatus of his soul and that that single performance forever modified his feelings about what life, with all its curious components, is.

When I had finished reading these words I paused and looked up at the ceiling. I thought of the iconic man's great chin-cleft and glorious moustache. I imagined him smiling into my eyes as a child, unfolding before me the unexpected structure of his story, surprising me with every turn of phrase and twist of the plot. And I thought about storytelling and how there isn't any way to construct an adequate description of what it is and what it does. And here, this boy's soul had marked clearly there was something illuminating in hearing the telling of a story. He had been so mesmerised by the experience that he was besotted and speechless as an adult in thinking of it. Well, then, I was one with Adrian Einhorn. I felt the same way and it was this kind of storytelling I needed to discover and impress upon my soul in that unventilated room in Hout Bay. Perhaps then there could be hope for my poetry performance, my students, and my pride. Because was this not indeed the problem: that none of us had ever seen, felt or smelled what a storytelling really was?

Of course, this was ridiculous because the thin threads of this kind of thinking were no basis to expect deliverance from the massive embarrassment which awaited me in that theatre on that dreaded date. I distracted myself from realistic thinking with a kind of desperation. I told myself that, somehow, by straining my body and wallet to invest in this venture, beneficent seeds would be sown for me. On the very morning we arrived in Cape Town, we made our way by a rented car to Hout Bay, and World of Birds Avenue number 23, where Mr Graves keeps his premises. Mr Graves, expecting my arrival, had cleared an old desk and set up a desk lamp upon it. He is a singular fellow, hatted and white-bearded, who lives alone by bravely maintaining a series of discourses, both with himself and with those who come temporarily within his sphere. It attracted my attention that he speaks in exactly the same kind of abstracted, detached mode, whether speaking to himself or another man, or whether moving from the former to the latter. He met me with a cordial smile, murmuring smoothly something about Kipling and the Royal Army. I nodded and expressed my gratitude, and he showed me with loudly creaking steps to my desk. On the desk I found ready and waiting the thin black volume entitled *My Rudyard Kipling*. Mr Graves told me he would make us a cup of tea.

Walter had gone off to explore Hout Bay. He had told me on the flight that he was originally Capetonian, his mother having moved the family to Johannesburg when Walter was six for work purposes. When I told him we were bound for Hout Bay he had jumped with excitement. He had many pleasant memories of Hout Bay beach and the fishing boats. 'The old rusty Hout Bay fishing boats,' he had repeated to himself several times. 'And the fish eateries and the fishing village,' he had also said. He had not seen all that for over thirty years. He instructed me to drop him anywhere near the harbour before parking at the library. He had alighted full of vim and walked off zipping up his leather jacket from the cold.

Now I sunk myself into Mr Einhorn's prose with an intensity built of months of pent-up stress. I found myself enwrapped in a surprising experience. The second chapter of the book was written clumsily and unprofessionally. In it, the author gushed forth with a rendition of his experience of that morning in November 1905 when the guest of honour at his school was Rudyard Kipling. Much of what he writes degenerates into emotional rambling. He speaks of the 'blessed spirit in the air – clear as daylight' when Kipling spoke. He writes that he felt, 'churning in my belly, from the moment Kipling entered the hall, the fearful perception that I was to meet the most pivotal life-guide I ever would encounter.'

I quoted in my notebook, though, the four instances in the chapter which hooked something in me. They read as follows:

1. Mr Kipling gave me the heartening feeling – and it is a monstrous gift I shed tears about receiving to this very day – that no matter if I would never see him again for the rest of my life, the fact of his existence meant everything in my life would be alright in the end.

2. In Mr Kipling's attitude of wisened enthusiasm for his subject matter – though it be an animal story – is somehow contained all of life.

3. In uttering each sonorous word, Mr Kipling mimicked the nature of the speaking spirit in its correct aspect and reminded me I was made to speak, to tell my own stories. And I knew from then on, as I know this very moment as I sit here in my chair, that as long as I speak and tell the story of what life is to me, of the pictures I see in it and the feelings it evokes for me, I shall be alive.

4. The period of my life during which Mr Kipling addressed us was one of acute distress and confusion for me personally. My parents' marriage was in a process of dissolution. I felt – I can remember quite clearly – afloat, terrified, and unloved at the prospect of the future and the sense that alliances I had believed were eternal bonds, might be loosened.

And in this challenging period, in walked Mr Kipling like my guardian angel. Though we all knew the story of Mowgli and Shere Khan he told was fiction, through his smile – that absolutely wondrous smile, obscured by his moustache but shining through every pore of his countenance, especially the area around his eyes – I received a message of rare comfort: "Adrian, wherever you go, I am not scared for you. I trust this old world to carry and keep your delicate body and soul because I know it's a good world."

5. Mr Kipling was demonstrating to me, in an act of secret kindness, that the world was a place I could tell the story of, that it was made to stand before me in obedience and to be understood by my mind. Life's events might be confusing at first but after taking a second glance, or after time, there was a story apparent to the eye. Each personality you encountered in life was placed there by design, to play a certain role or to allow you to play a certain role, and then it would make way for the next.

Now, it was manifest that Mr Einhorn's reaction was personal and, as he admits, he happened to be in a sensitive state at the time of the performance. But as I read and re-read the five passages I had penned in my notebook, a different impression, one quite unexpected, settled with me and it was this impression that was causing a tingly stir in my abdomen. It was the impression that, when all had been said, Adrian Einhorn was a special little boy whose soul was touched by what the famous gentleman worked in that school hall on that morning. The other boys and the staff had not been touched. If I chose to sit in my wooden chair in Hout Bay on this morning, many mornings later, and judge him as frivolous, I was no different to them. His potential to be touched was a blessing, an advantage, not a disqualifying blemish. I saw Adrian Einhorn sitting cross-legged on the cold school-hall floor. I watched his wide-open eyes as waves of emotion, invisible to the others present, pulsed beneath them. I was more one with him than with them. His infatuation signified there was life in him. His pure mind was not dulled by cynicism. Besides, he was a kindred spirit: he was impassioned by speech performance and so was I.

So it was that I sat in that musty little room feeling positively that miracles had been done for me. Some might argue that I had wilfully deluded myself in order to manufacture hope, but I say otherwise. And the enchantment that hung over me emanated from these precious fragments of fact, which showed there had been an event – many events – passed by and taken for granted in their own time but which were highly significant. The ancient power of speech had been openly demonstrated. Those whose souls were numb perceived nothing in it, and there always were those whose souls were numb. If I had been there – if *I* had been there! – I should have done or become . . . I don't know what, in the course of my life. Perhaps I should have become a travelling story-teller, to adults and children alike. Perhaps I would be filled with life and would be making warm, beneficent marks on the lives of my students, so *my* smile would be impressed upon their memories forever. I am a believer in daydreaming, so I perpetuated these fancies in quiet excitement for some hours, dipping into my quotes from Einhorn to be refreshed, and adding my notes on Einhorn's phrases, trying to capture what his experience would have been if it had been mine.

For seven days I sat in 23 World of Birds Road, reading onward in Einhorn, contemplating sketches of Kipling, and closing my eyes and watching the performance of a lifetime in my own primary school hall. I also went for walks in a state of heavy reverie, saying over phrases to myself. Walter and I only met for lunch and in the evening. I was surprised to see that he was full of a happy energy due mainly to the sea breeze and the fishing boats, of which he did not tire but kept on praising with his lips and circling with his feet.

It had seemed to me before that he was intimately attached to the city life, so this was unexpected.

On the eighth day after our arrival, Walter told me he was going to rise early the following morning to join the crew of a fishing boat on their day's work. I saw him at five o'clock that evening when he separated from a group of six fishermen standing around a great net full of fish and chatting easily in the ripening colours of dusk. He met me in what seemed like a state of deep relaxation.

'How was it?' I asked.

'Some days go well. Some go less well,' he told me. 'But we don't complain.'

The next day he informed me he was going to stay in a room nearer the harbour that night so as to make it easier to meet the boat on time before dawn. Then I was deprived of his company for three consecutive days. Growing concerned, I questioned a fishing crew about his whereabouts. One of the group directed me to a different crew and from one of these men I received an assurance I would be guided to meet Walter when he would be leaving the docks in fifteen minutes. He walked with me into the fishing village on the hill opposite Hout Bay harbour. This is a collection of old blocks of flats and a smattering of small houses surrounded by low rusty gates. We walked into a street consisting mainly of these houses, past a mangy brown dog that barked at us, and then my guide opened the rusty gate of one of the houses. Through the neglected garden we walked and he opened the front door. He looked around the house after we entered, and, seeing nothing but peeling walls, missing bricks and a torn folding chair, turned to his right and entered a small kitchen. I followed him into this tiny room and there sat Walter by a tattered kitchen table, doing nothing but grip a large tin mug of steaming tea. He looked up and, marking us both, merely nodded in greeting.

I sat down at the table. My guide bade us farewell and left. Walter was possessed of a weary aspect and was dressed in the white overalls of a Hout Bay fisherman. The odour of fish hung distinctly upon his clothes. I waited and watched him. He, who seemed half in a dream from weariness, roused himself by rocking himself mildly in a full-body nod. He sipped his tea relishingly.

'Ya, brother, how are you?' he asked thickly.

'I am fantastic, thank you,' said I. 'And how have things been going for you?'

'It's a good life, brother,' he said. 'And we don't complain. We don't complain.' And he rocked himself on. The most notable aspect of Walter was that he seemed content with sitting in his place lethargically and sipping his tea. Another thing attracted my attention, though. I noticed when he spoke there was something unusual about his mouth. I couldn't help but stare, so I was forced to explain myself.

'Walter, you are missing all of your front teeth!' I said.

He raised a weary eyebrow from eyes that watched his mug, saying:

'Ya, brother. That's the way it's done here.'

'Is it really?' I asked. 'You knocked out, you removed, your own front teeth?'

'Ya,' he said lowly. 'In the village that's the way it's done.'

'Why?' I asked.

'It's the custom,' he answered. He looked out the window, not as if to indicate he was disinterested but rather in blank curiosity, as though the sight of the white sunlight playing on the dust in the air might accord with what he had expected to see or might not, but both were equal to him. He sipped his tea noisily and dropped his head on his chest. The minutes ticked by.

'Walter,' I said, 'I must say, it seems to me rather surprising to see you here.'

He gazed at me open-mouthed, revealing his bare gums and palate.

'Ya?' he said. 'Why is that, brother?' Yes, his accent was decidedly different, I thought. There could be no doubt on the point. 'Th' had become 'd'. 'Aw' had become 'ah'.

'Well,' I said, 'you seem to have set up house here and adopted the life of a fisherman.'

'Ya,' said Walter, his gums still available for the view.

'The reason it surprises me,' I said gently, 'is that I didn't realise this was a lifestyle with which you felt familiar at all.'

'Oh,' he said, less confused. 'It *is*, brother. It *is*. As I told you, my ma used to live in Hout Bay with us when we was small. I know this place from . . . since I was a . . . little pikkie,' and he gave me the broadest smile I could wish for, yet it lacked something.

'For me,' he continued, gazing around with a sudden grin, 'this place is bread and butter. You understand? My first bread and butter. It's like coming home. Ya, my brother, I wouldn't want to be *any*where else. Ha ha ha.'

I showed him with a smile I understood what he meant. He enjoyed the warm thought. From appearances, there was a humour, true philosophy and raw feeling, all three contained within this thought. When all these trailed off into silence, the minutes began to tick away again.

'Well,' I said, 'now that I know where you live, I can come visit you more often.'

'*Absolutely*, my brother,' he said, lighting up at my phrases, and offered me his hand. I took it firmly and showed him the smile of friendly comradery. This seemed to keep him lit up, fending off the descent of that heavy lethargy in consciousness.

'No, don't see me out,' I said. 'There's no need for formality among friends!'

'Alright, brother,' he said, chuckling, 'since it's friends we are, I'll stay here and I won't see you out.' This is how I left him and, believe me when I tell you, I don't believe a man has walked that dilapidated dust street back to the harbour while shedding tears with such a profound sorrow.

Following this came a period when the screws of the machine of life were tightened. I was in telephone contact with Mrs Sabukwana who asked for a report of Walter's status. I for my part found myself ill-prepared to answer the question with the subtle mixture of eva-siveness, hopefulness and honesty that was required. I stumbled over my first words but then found my footing slightly by telling her Walter had responded with great enthusiasm to Hout Bay and was presently benefiting from the tender memories he associated with the little suburb. To this she listened with a closeness but I detected something new in her quavering voice: something which lay behind her long silences and short responses. Out of my impa-tience for new obscurity I questioned her directly: was there some-thing bothering her?

'No, it's nothing,' she said, 'only that I was overwhelmed by something – by a conversation I had the day before yesterday. It was a conversation with Doctor Tobias. He phones me often to check up on me. He told me I shouldn't hope for any miracles because it's a waste of my emotions and I'm sure to be disappointed. But then afterwards he said something which has . . . been playing on my mind and disturbing me.'

What was this?

'If I understood correctly, he proposed marriage to me.'

I was dumbfounded. The foulness of this man had struck me before but somehow eluded my clear recognition.

'Jane,' I said, 'listen to me. You are a married woman. Your hus-band is going to return to you. Give him the chance to recover, to find himself again. Think of all the years you have shared together, all the memories. Are they something you feel comfortable just throwing away? I'm telling you I see very promising signs; there's no question about it. All I need is a little more time. You need to practice patience and wait for my call. I promise you, if I recognise that hope is gone, I'll tell you honestly. I won't hide it. But then you would have to be open and upfront with Walter, to warn him before-hand. You can't ignore him as if he weren't really a person. For this Tobias to speak that way with you now is ridiculously inappropriate.'

She agreed with me but in a weak voice and seemed distinctly unsubstantial. I could not say much more that would help now but

I felt uncomfortable hanging up the phone because that detestable creature was going to persist in contacting her. I entreated her as a last thought not to listen to Doctor Tobias and even to refuse to speak to him. A flurry of emotion forced her to beg my apology and hang up.

On the afternoon of the very same day I was speaking with my colleague from the University of Cape Townwho mentioned there was a crisis on campus. A student had climbed to the roof of her dormitory building in order, she claimed, to throw herself off. She would not move from her spot and screamed when anyone would approach. She had not moved from the roof for a day and a half. Her responses to the negotiators who had been sent were minimal. Mostly she ignored their words and simply hugged herself, gazing down to the ground below. I felt positively awful. I asked, had she told the reason for all this to anyone? My colleague answered that all she had said was:

'No one cares. No one cares.'

What could be done? There were gathering rainclouds on all fronts. I felt the weight of foreboding in my chest, which began to feel asthmatic. I went for a run in the cold sea air near evening time.

My run took me to Walter's district where, on a whim, I paid him a visit. He answered the door in a stunned mood which comes from imbibing hours of silence. I asked him, could I accompany him to work the following day – since this was something he knew I enjoyed doing? He answered yes, and that tomorrow he was working behind the counter of the fishery.

At 3.25 am I was wide awake. I needed to feel the freezing air unwarmed by land and inhabitation. I needed to escape the intimidating questions which kept intruding upon my mind. I needed to shake off my dreams of the future and locate the present moment once again.

I was ready outside the doors of the fishery when Walter and five other workers clad in white plastic aprons and white boots opened the shop doors. I followed them into the freezing room that smelled potently of fish, so much so that I could barely stand it. Walter slapped icy water all over his arms up to the elbows, dried them on a large white towel hanging on a hook, and pulled on a thick pair of plastic gloves. To one of the lady workers busying herself behind the counter who happened to pass him, Walter cheerfully sung the first verse of the Afrikaans song:

Goeie more my vrou, hier's 'n soentjie vir jou.

[Good morning my wife, here's a kiss for you.]

And he puckered his lips as if to do so. She answered with the next verse, and pointing with her thumb to their kettle behind her.

Goeie more my man, daar is koffie in die kan.

[Good morning my husband, there's coffee in the can.]

And both, as well as another worker behind the counter, cackled in full-body laughter for a short while. I am able to make myself very inconspicuous, which I did expertly for the next hours. I wondered at Walter, who massaged the scaly bodies of fish as if there were nothing more natural in the world. He operated a knife to gut a fish as though he were buttering his toast. The innards – he placed in the appropriate tub without the slightest look of revulsion. A bead of sweat on his forehead – he wiped away expertly with his shoulder. After this he squinted open-mouthed up at the clock, revealing the red of his gums, to check how long until opening time.

Then he called out in a voice that carried powerfully through the spacious tiled room:

'So where is this coffee you're telling me about, Sallie?'

There were cries of assent from further behind the counter. The shop opened for business and Walter inclined himself forward to better hear the requests of customers. A lady of middle age requested yellowtail. Walter told her there was none available for the day, but also:

'You know, everyone wants the yellowtail, but I think it's very bony. The kabeljou is delicious, not bony, and much cheaper.'

The lady agreed to accept a kilo of kabeljou instead of the yellowtail. Walter went to work carving it into portions of the desired size. Behind the glass, on a bed of ice, lay a pile of angelfish; four or five giant snoek; several hake; a red roman; a large bunch of mussels; and a big red lobster. The customers began to enter steadily and their expressions became more excited when they viewed the display.

As it approached twelve, Walter reached down into a great box of raw mussels, took one, and while turning slightly aside, sucked it out of its shell with an audible slurping. It slid unobstructed over his palate and down his throat. He repeated this performance several times with the attitude of one dusting off his coat.

A lady customer complained that the way Walter had packaged her order was not correct. She had asked for four separate half-kilo portions of skinned salmon, and Walter had given her two-kilo portions of unskinned salmon. Walter listened, holding onto the packages, but not budging to make any alteration. Said the lady now in a tone of heightened intolerance:

'Are you understanding me? Do you speak English? I will not accept that because it's not what I ordered.'

Here my chest was aflutter, as it did any time rebuke seemed to threaten Walter. I dreaded this because I knew from experience Walter did not go well together with rebuke. The poisonous little woman persisted in spurting her terrible speech.

'Maybe you should call someone who can understand the customers. Where's the manager?'

Little did this troll of a woman know she was tampering with universes that hung on the beat of a ladybug's wings. Whatever could be said about Walter's state of late, and I was not at all certain what that would be, he was at least merry. He was thriving – that was apparent. Any fool who had happened to drag himself along to observe what I had of his story up to this point knew that now he should be left alone. I considered that the gutting knives lay very conveniently on the counter. Walter had been holding the packages of fish, dumbly looking down at the woman. But now I was further baffled by the one-of-a-kind man. He spoke now with clarity and volume, but composedly.

'Just wait a minute, Lady,' he said. 'The way you are talking to me is not right. It's not the way human beings talk to human beings. Over here we serve people if those people treat others in the way they would like to be treated. People who don't should shop somewhere else.'

A lady customer called out:

'He's right!' The little terrier of a woman, though, called again for the manager.

'No, I'm not calling any manager,' said Walter. 'The manager agrees with me. You can come back here when you are ready to treat people with respect.'

Exasperated, the woman threw up a hand and left. There were a few calls of support for Walter. I saw his hand was steady as can be, though in the police station some weeks ago it had trembled severely. He accepted a congratulations from Sallie with dignity and promptly received his next customer. I was in awe at him.

The afternoon wore on. Walter adjusted the fish and poured new ones onto the ice. He was replaced by a fellow worker long enough to take a tea break, and withdrew to the rear to sit on a stool, drinking tea and eating biscuits. He turned on the radio as he munched and listened closely to some discussion on Afrikaans talk radio. He heard something said which brought him to cry out loudly for all to assemble and listen. The other workers gathered, wrought themselves uncomfortably, and inclined their ears to the muffled talk emitting from the small black radio. When two minutes of this had passed, Walter looked up at them all with an expression of the most passionate alacrity and, pointing at the machine with his index finger, burst into fits of laughter which gave rise to more of the same in those gathered. The laughter was piercing and Walter's eyes filled with tears. I found this, for reasons having to do with my own sensibility, a subject for fascination.

Walter was mopping the floor at the day's end. I stood out the way and he did not speak but only drew the mop back and forth, forth and back.

'A good group of people they are – your co-workers, I mean,' I said.

'Ya, absolutely they are,' he said. 'The best people are Hout Bay people.'

He mopped on, adding nothing, for several minutes.

'That little woman who was complaining, then, must not be a Hout Bay person,' I said.

'Oh! Let me tell you something,' said Walter, 'a lady can grow up in the best schools and universities, and think she is so refined, but doesn't know how to treat a person. It's a fact.'

'I really believe it is,' I said. Walter wrung out his mop in a big green bucket and reapplied it to the floor. Back and forth, forth and back he mopped but didn't raise his head for ten minutes.

'You must be exhausted after this day!' I said.

'Me? No, I'm strong,' he said, holding his mop. 'Anyway, I get my energy, I get my happiness from the work itself. I like working with the guys. I like joking around with them. I like making conversation with the customers. That's me, the way I am.'

'Well they're lucky to have a bubbly, sociable worker like you,' I said.

'Ya, Hout Bay people are the best people,' he said.

Back and forth he mopped, progressing to the rear of the shop as he went, not minding me. I myself was a bit dizzy from standing for so many hours and lack of nourishment, so perhaps it was for that reason that here my sensibility became piqued.

'The best people, absolutely', I said. 'Not like a certain lady we met today in the shop.'

'Let me just tell you something,' said Walter, holding his mop. 'Someone can get the best education and think that makes them a good person, but they don't know how to treat a person with basic respect. Do you know what I mean?'

'Yes I do, absolutely,' I said. Walter, who was mopping with incredible stamina, in five minutes had almost come full circle in the room back to me.

'Walter,' I said, 'tell me, do you like this kind of work?'

'Ah! yes, man,' he said. 'Just joking around with the guys and talking with them and the customers, that's what I like. And that's what gives me energy for the day. That's the way I am.'

The worn nerves, the late hour, or both, were bringing something into the open. No one was present to witness it but me. A stray cat curled itself around my leg, inquiring about the question of leftover scraps.

'Walter,' I said, 'Do we have any leftovers for this nice cat?'

'Ya, we do,' he said. He grabbed a gloved handful of offcuts from a large plastic box and carried it to the door, where I stood, and lay it down just outside in the cat's bowl. As he was about to return to his work, I held him by the sleeve and he stopped, looking up with a question.

'Do you get many ladies around here like that one who was here today?' I asked.

He lapsed into a grin.

'Can I tell you something?' he said. 'Someone can go their whole life thinking they're the bee's knees but if you ask them how do you treat someone with respect, they won't be able to answer you. I'm serious. I don't know if you believe me – I can see the way you're looking at me – but I'm serious.'

'No, I believe you,' I said. 'I believe it.'

'Their whole life they can go like that,' he said. 'That's why I like Hout Bay people. They're straight and simple. They're the best people.'

Tomorrow, Walter was going fishing and I wanted to come along. He told me on which pier to be waiting at 4:30 am. The fishing boat was rusty in the extreme. I waited to board over the gangplank in icy air and in no more light than that provided by a faint orange glow over the horizon. Our team of fishermen didn't feel the need to greet me but only rubbed their hands together and blew upon them. I mustered the bravery to cross over the rotten piece of wood and was incorporated into the ranks of these sturdy men who called out to each other gutturally. I felt so exposed emotionally due to the events of yesterday and the previous weeks that I found Walter directly and warmly shook his hand.

'I'm fortunate to have a friend like you!' I called out to him against the choppy air and the beating sails.

He smiled generously.

'*I* am the lucky one to have *you* as a friend,' he said.

The boat romped over the rows of low waves that kept appearing from somewhere in the distance, rising and crashing. Our vessel was not proud but it had durability on its side. Our captain took us far out to sea so the sight of Hout Bay was lost to us. All that surrounded us was the churn of disturbed waters, white and foamy, which also seemed bitter at being forced to work in such cold weather.

The rough old brown nets were hurled out without fanfare. Larger swells rocked us in a slow rhythm, down then up. And a great spray whipped me across the face, invigorating me with fresh spirit. Walter eyed me to ensure I was well and I reassured him with a smile. Then he surprised me by drawing close and calling out to me.

'John,' said Walter, 'you are troubled.'

'Troubled?' I said, 'Yes, I'm troubled.'

'What's the matter?' he asked.

My mind ran over a couple of matters I preferred not to mention.

'Actually, I'm not troubled. I have a question I want to ask you, though. Do you ever get seasick?'

'Never!' he said. 'For me this is no different to being on land.'

'That's unusual,' I said. 'Hasn't it been years since you've been on a boat?'

'It's as I explained to you,' he said. 'All of it is part of my mind, part of my memory from my childhood. I played with fishing boats instead of dinky cars. My friends and I spent our afternoons making boats.'

'That was many years ago,' I said.

'Still,' he said, 'the feeling of being on a boat, the sights, the smells, are familiar. When I arrived here I felt I was slotting back in.'

I looked over my shoulder at the other fishermen.

'Do you feel any different to them?'

'Not much,' he said.

One of the fishermen began pouring hot brandy from a flask into tin mugs for each of us.

'But the kinds of food they eat; the kinds of drink they drink must be unfamiliar,' I said to Walter.

'Not really,' he said. 'I remember. My palate remembers. And let me tell you something else. When I arrived back here, I felt returning here was the real reason I chose to have the operation done. I was always in love with the life here deep inside, but the love was lost. I knew the operation would open me up to that love. Now I feel . . . in love again, really in love.' And he sipped his brandy heartily.

'I see,' I said. The boat rocked in the choppy waters.

'But I told you,' I said on an impulse, 'the doctor's report was a mistake. He admitted it was a mistake. It could be the operation had no effect at all.'

'It had no bad effect, maybe,' he said. 'I know it had a good effect.'

'How do you know?'

'I can feel!' he said. 'It feels like I was asleep for so many years, and now I'm awake again. It feels like I've been eating and drinking for all these years without knowing what I'm doing, like a sleep-walker. Now for the first time since I was a kid I'm eating again, I'm drinking again.'

'That sounds wonderful, Walter,' I said. He showed me his gums, the little concavities where his front teeth had been, still red.

'Well then, I'm concerned for myself!' I said. 'Perhaps I'm not really eating, not really drinking.'

He shrugged. The boat bounced up sharply and slapped down on the water. He looked around with a mild expression of concern, open-mouthed. His eyes were chocolate brown.

It was time for Walter to help haul in the nets. As he did so, the sun lit up the grey hairs on the sides of his head. His muscles were tough and stringy, and the loose skin under his biceps did nothing to diminish his strength. More pulling power was needed to lug the catch into the air and on board. All the men applied themselves. Finally the catch came into view, squirming and wriggling in immense silvery life, and was laid on deck. Walter regarded it as he would something mundane. The sun had come out in its full strength for the moment, as if in celebration of the catch. My gaze was drawn by some particular fish, struggling dumbly, flipping this way and that. This fish's scales, abruptly exposed to the sunlight to sparkle for my eyes, somehow embarrassed me so I turned away.

On the way back Walter hung onto a cable, listening to one of the men tell a story. He glared out to the bay with a broad expression of glee. Behind him on the deck many of the fish were still moving, but the music of the story, the music of the boat rising and sinking as it progressed, was holding onto his mind. A great hiss emanated from the ocean expanse. Walter hearkened to it with satisfaction. To my ears it soon faded into the background.

Our vessel was drifting into place in the docks. Walter and the other men rushed and tugged and tightened in well-attuned unison. An old man wearing a Panama hat stood on the pier with a golden retriever observing our arrival through sunglasses. As our routine preparations progressed, he watched with a consuming interest and the dog was forced to restrain himself to stand with his master. On deck, the catch came into his view: among the silvery cluster, a crayfish moving its feelers and a small swordfish. The dog barked at the catch but the man didn't move. We were at rest long enough that the commotion of our arrival was forgotten, and the man moved on in an unconvinced fashion, the dog following.

Walter had crossed the gangplank and stood in big plastic boots on the concrete pier surveying the work at hand. I also crossed to shore and looked back down onto the deck. The certain movements of the fishermen were like the steps of a spider on its web, something curious to my thought-worn mind, which had ceased its cogitating long enough to look out and see it. I allowed my mind to follow the movements of their dark figures, thus finding forgetfulness from its chain of obtuse frustrations. The sun dawned in fuller strength.

I gave up on my plans for the day and simply hung onto the trail of the fishermen. Mid-morning we all moved on to the home of Paul, one of the fishermen. Canned pilchards and porridge were cooking in his kitchen. Paul's wife nursed an injury on his heel after he ate. When she applied alcohol to the wound, I saw him wince in pain. The men were given small tin cups of condensed milk for dessert.

Paul's son, a young teenager, arrived and a bowl of porridge was wordlessly laid out for him. He conducted himself with reserve and politeness. After lunch he went to the back garden where he kept a vegetable patch and tended to his spinach and carrots. His mother chatted to him as she hung the wet laundry on the line. Her younger son kneeled in the yard, playing with a toy bicycle made of wire.

A little girl from a neighbouring home then arrived and began arranging a game of hide-and-seek. She sang and clapped as she went and some other children appeared in the yard and began dancing in a circle with her. She acted out a farewell, waving goodbye and then falling down in tears, her hands nestling in her lap. Then she would rise and act out a joyous greeting, spinning around smoothly as she embraced an invisible someone. The toddler began mimicking her motions as she revolved around the yard, and the toddler's mother left her laundry to do the same. I joined in too, so there was a train of us following her lead in the white light and quickening breeze of the late morning. We would join hands and separate at her lead, and when she did separate she would act out hunger, only to be fed by her neighbour, who in turn would be fed by her. I went round, clinging to my heart in despair, demonstrating the pitter-patter of tears with my fingertips, winding around and through a rusty jungle gym in a sandpit. We danced through autumn, when the leaves reddened and browned and made a soft bed on which we could walk. Winter came and we had to huddle and warm our hands by fires. We met streams and rapids through which we were forced to swim. Over rickety bridges we walked, one after the other. We grew old and died and mourned for ourselves for months. We were reborn very fragile as if for the first time, knowing nothing of the seasons and tastes of things. We tottered into the future with the ignorance of a toddler; rushed each to the other's rescue to carry him to safety; and we finally joined in a massive embrace and fell to the ground in one motion.

'Walter, I need help,' I told that man when I had recovered from the dance and the heat of the afternoon had set in. 'I'm afraid I'm going to be embarrassed. My students are going to give a performance of storytelling in a theatre and I have to instruct them how a story should be told. There was a man who knew how to tell stories wonderfully well, and there was a boy who was present on one occasion when he told a story. He tells about what he remembers of the performance of the great storyteller in a book he wrote. I need you to listen to what he says and help me feel what it felt like to be in that boy's shoes on that day. I need to see what he saw. I know it may sound funny, but will you sit with me in the library for a bit and listen to his words?'

Walter, who had been a careful listener, cocked his brow somewhat to show surprise but agreed with a slight nod.

He arrived at the library wearing thick home-knit clothing of rough texture. Mr Graves assumed he was misdirected and met him with cold confusion, but I assured him the man was with me. Mr Graves made apologies and returned to the kettle. There was a one-seater couch for Walter, who, with the passing of minutes, seemed bashfully to draw enjoyment from the warm room, the cosy occupation that was to be ours, and the hot tea. I told him of Adrian Einhorn and my five quotes from his pen. And I asked him to listen carefully while I read out the first quote. He closed his eyes and lay his head back on the couch while listening. He asked me to repeat it when I had finished. Then I continued to read all five quotes. He seemed particularly affected by the fourth quote, which discusses Einhorn's reaction to the end of his parents' marriage. This he asked me to repeat three or four times.

'Shoo!' he said when I had finished, 'what a man Kipling was! I can see him. I tell you, I can just see him. What a man!'

I told Walter:

'You don't need to imagine. I'll show you. Look at these pictures.'

I showed him a series of large pictures and he stopped on one in particular which depicts the gentleman as a young man gazing out the window with a smile.

'Now I can *really* see him,' said Walter. 'How I would love to hear him tell his stories!'

'Me too,' said I, 'believe me.'

'I want you to tell me one of his stories,' said Walter.

'You're welcome to read any of them you like,' I said. 'They're all here.'

'No, I prefer you read to me,' he said.

I bent to peruse a shelf near my knees. My eyes rested on an old red hardcover edition of *The Second Jungle Book* which I presently removed. I found the opening of the first of the stories, called 'How Fear Came'. Without so much as a hesitating thought I began reading. I read about the Law of the Jungle, that ancient law which every law-abiding animal respects, and which always triumphs in the end.

'I know what he's talking about,' said Walter with his eyes closed. 'He's talking about the world. The world – this old old world has seen *plenty* up till today and everybody is connected and everything goes on according to plan, although *we* plan differently.'

My ears pricked up, I noticed, as did all the flesh on my back and chest in goose pimples. But in the forgotten room, none knew me or heard me but Walter Sabukwana, Now I read on all about Mowgli the wolf-boy who grew tired of the lessons given him in the Law by Baloo the Brown Bear. He felt he had no need for lessons, since he knew enough of the Jungle already.

'Ho ho!' said Walter. 'Do you hear what he's saying now? The young boy thinks he knows the ways of the world. He's sure as sure can be. He walks around proudly as if those much older knew only a small part of what he knows. And only with time does he see he is really empty of knowledge and understanding. Only when winter passes and then spring and summer, and around again, and some days there's a big catch and some days there's almost nothing. And his skin becomes hard and worn by the cold and drying air. Then it starts to sink into his thick skull. There's a way things work and you have to open your heavy ears to hear or you'll never learn.'

Now my every pore was taut with the conviction that my flesh had been laid upon my bones in order to experience this moment. I continued reading. Walter heard about the failure of the winter rains, when Ikki the Porcupine warned Mowgli that the wild yams were drying up. Mowgli was still confident in his ability to hunt out all he needed from the jungle.

'Ha ha!' said Walter. '"Ikki" – what a name! That's the name of the porcupine. I like that.'

Ikki proved that the drought was dire by pointing to the shallow rock-pool. If Mowgli were to dive into it, he'd crack his head, but, then again, that might let in some wisdom.

'Ha ha ha!' screamed Walter. 'That is wonderful. That is brilliant. Isn't it exactly like I said? His head is hard because in youth every boy's head is hard. It's hard to get even a *drop* of knowledge into there. But there's a drought. The older animals know all about droughts from their years of experience, but to him it doesn't even exist. He is going to have his food – the way he has been accustomed, and his drink – the way he has been accustomed, every day of his life. That is the way he feels. Why not? Why shouldn't things continue the way they always have for me? That is the way he feels. But he has a surprise waiting for him because life doesn't go like that. It's sad that he doesn't know that, that he won't hear that.'

Walter's mood calibrated with this notion perfectly. He was sober and lucid. I wouldn't look up from my text. I read to Walter about the coming of the famine and how Chil the Kite was the only one of the jungle animals to grow fat, on carrion. Walter shook his head and smiled a bitter smile with eyes that twinkled. Onward I pushed, telling how Mowgli met the experience of hunger for the first time, and that he was forced to eat stale black honey and dry sugar.

Now Walter shook his head again and his cheeks were moist with tears.

'Foolish boy,' he stuttered weakly. 'He's finding out the way things go, isn't he? Yes he is.'

Mr. Graves rose from his own reading to walk over and peek in on our little corner of the room with a worried look, but he moved on when I shot him back my best evil eye. Next, Walter listened to the great event of the Water-truce, when Hathi the Elephant saw that the rock-pool was so depleted that Peace Rock was visible. He trumpeted his declaration of the Water-Truce, which is the agreement the animals make, in such times, that all may drink at the rock-pool without fear of being hunted.

Walter's cheeks were warmed by an emotion of deep orange. I spied the changes of expression darting over his face greedily but never openly.

'If even Hathi,' said Walter, 'that hundred-year-old ancient elephant sees this is an unusual time, then it must be a special time. But don't forget, it has happened before in the days of Hathi's father. It's not the first time. It's only that you have to be ancient like Hathi to see the larger patterns in things. Hathi is not panicked. He just knows it's the time when we call the Water Truce. And there are times like that. Ay! And what a thing is the Water Truce! It shows we really are all brothers, working together to keep this lovely old world going. I play the panther, you play the springbok, but in the end we are bound together in one. It's like the sea and the fish. The sea is empty without the fish. The fish has no home without the sea. That's me and you.'

I felt myself witnessing this and, as I sat on my heavy wooden chair, I knew that I myself had played no active part in the dynamics of these events. Miracles were being wrought and I was nothing but a piece of furniture before the powerful forces that were operating. Then I noticed something else had been accomplished by an extraneous force: an idea had been planted in my mind. It had a certain feeling associated with it – a feeling of outlandish excitement. It was alive and drew life organically from the soil of my inner terrain in the way of a plant. It was also burnished and complete of itself. I was watching it in the quiet of the room, but presently I attempted listening to it. It said as follows: Let us bring together Walter with the suicidal student to bring about salvation. Such a surprising message, I felt. It may be fancy, or nonsense, yet it was certainly intriguing.

Because, as I have said, one of my plentiful failings is the tendency to be drawn after fanciful possibilities, I was now filled with adrenaline. I clung tightly onto the arms of my chair and called out to Mr Graves that I needed to use his telephone urgently. The poor gentleman hastily guided me to an old black telephone that sat near the tea corner. I took the receiver and dialled the office number of my colleague at UCT. Thank goodness he answered and I asked him if anything had changed regarding the situation of the pitiful student on the rooftop. He told me that as of now all was the same. Feeling doubtfully silly, I heard myself telling him I was on my way to campus with what may be her salvation, and I asked him could he meet me at his office in fifteen minutes to guide me to the young lady.

We rushed off in my Toyota and on the way I explained to Walter about the urgency that was calling for our presence. He was very sympathetic but questioned me in his simple way as to how it was *we* who were able to save the poor girl. I told him he need not worry about that because it would become clear when we arrived, and then told myself the same thing, and I filled my mind with the mechanics of driving as speedily as safety would allow. We arrived on campus and then trotted hastily to my colleague Brian Wilson's office. After a knock, he called to enter. When we did, he began to question me but in my breathlessness I cut him short.

'Brian, we'll explain later. There's no time now. This is Walter Sabukwana. He's my friend. Take us, I beg you, to the young lady. No time to waste. We may be able to do something for her.'

Brian, to his credit, dropped everything and led the way out onto Campus Boulevard. It was not a long walk down four flights of stairs to the ladies' dormitory, where we entered past the security guard at Brian's word. We ascended all eighteen flights of steps to the roof of the building. Out we came into light and fresh air, finally, our hearts pumping vigorously. Our eyes didn't need to search far to find her. Her figure could immediately be seen sitting cross-legged near the edge of the roof. She was facing the edge and hugged herself tenderly, but was still. When we had walked several steps towards her, she turned her head to look in our direction. She said nothing but only watched as we warily stepped on towards her.

'Stop!' she called out as if weary of the word. 'Stay there.' We obeyed. She looked away from us, over the edge again, filled with a thoroughly weary spirit. I called out to her.

'Young lady! Hello! My name is John Legrand. I don't know you but I have heard about you. I wanted very much to come speak with you for just a few moments if you will allow.' She said nothing and did not move.

'I am not a brilliant man. I am not a man of powerful words. So you don't need to worry that I will try to convince you of anything. I only came to do two simple things and then I will go on my way and not bother you anymore. The first thing is to tell you I also have been young like you, and felt alone like you, and, though I didn't feel exactly like you feel, I have felt something similar. And I let things roll on and they got much better in the end. And the second thing is to introduce you to my friend Walter.' Nothing changed at first, but soon she looked in our direction again.

'You might be wondering,' I continued, 'why it's so important to me that you meet Walter. Well, I'll tell you. There's a very good reason, I felt, why you should meet Walter. Walter is the best storyteller in the world. I personally love hearing stories be told, and I thought maybe you were the same. So I brought him to you. I'm sure you have never heard anything like his stories.'

The still air on the roof hung and shifted listlessly like an audience waiting for a performance to begin. We saw her neck straighten now and we heard her female voice plaintively crossing the stony unused terrain.

'What kind of stories does he tell?' she was saying.

'Oh!' I said. 'You'll have to hear in order to know. There's no way for me to explain.' Brian was looking from the young lady to myself and back again in abject wonder. I went over to Walter and told him as follows:

'Walter, what I think the young lady needs is to hear the story of "How Fear Came" just as you told it in the library. Can you show her that? She would so enjoy it. It would warm her heart.'

Walter, who until now had been observing evenly, turned from me to step a few paces closer to the young woman.

'Young Sissie!' said Walter, 'I just heard a story that filled me with wonder and my friend John wants me to share it with you.

'Now, the story starts like this: the first thing you have to know before even hearing what will happen is that this world with its Laws is old old old. People and families have lived a hundred years ago and two hundred years ago and more, and planned their plans and been disappointed and died. And their children have grown up and done the same. That's because it's a world where the Laws of the world will dominate; not the laws in man's mind. We cannot see them most of the time because we're stuck in our small space, but if you look at a long span of time, you will see the Law dominates and there's no way of getting around that. That's the first thing.'

Walter had started in a diffident manner but was growing comfortable and voluble, and he began to pace back and forth and make use of his hands.

'But now you're ready to hear about Mowgli. There was a boy named Mowgli. This boy – you won't believe this – grew up in the jungle among the animals. He never had a human mother. Can you believe that?'

We watched the dear girl and she sat absolutely stationary gazing at Walter.

'This boy, because he was young and had no experience in life, believed he knew much more than the other animals in the jungle, even those who were older and more experienced than him. He felt in his heart, whatever I know is all there is to know. Whatever I am used to, is the way things will continue forever. What can you do? It's the way of the youth the world over. But listen to what happened next. Ikki the porcupine–'

'Who?' the girl asked.

'Ikki,' said Walter. 'That's the name of one of the porcupines in the jungle. He tried one day to explain in a very kind way to Mowgli that, although the boy was so full of confidence in his way of viewing things, things would keep on their tracks as they were, and truthfully a famine was coming. The signs of it were already all over the jungle. The rivers had dried up and the trees and plants were dying. But Mowgli, being young, would not see the truth of what was developing before his eyes. He kept on walking around proudly with a big proud smile on his face as if he ruled the jungle. But eventually he could not blind himself to the facts as they came along. The trees Mowgli normally fed from dried up and he ate – do you know what he had to eat? – dried up blackened sugar!'

'Really?' asked the girl.

'Yes!' answered Walter. 'He did!

'But keep listening to what happened next. Hathi was the great ancient elephant who ruled the jungle and had seen many summers and winters pass. He raised up his giant trunk and trumpeted out to the animals of the jungle. And do you know what it was that he trumpeted?'

'What?' she asked.

'That there was going to be a Water Truce.'

'What?' she asked.

'A Water Truce. I'll tell you what it means. It means that normally the leopard chases the springbok and the crocodile hunts the warthog, but sometimes – once in every fifty years at the most – water becomes so scarce that all the animals actually make an agreement that there will not be any hunting, so that the springbok and the warthog can drink at the watering hole without worrying about an attack.'

Walter's voice projection had been natural and impressive. We looked to the young lady. She sat absolutely still, indecipherable.

'The leopard would drink right next to the warthog, and the lioness right next to the springbok,' continued Walter. 'And here's the question everyone asks about the Water Truce: why do they make this agreement?'

'Why?' she asked.

'Here's the secret, young Sissie,' said Walter. 'But here you have to listen. Because each one of the animals is part of one whole. Not only does the leopard need the springbok, but the springbok needs the leopard. Why? Because without the leopard chasing him, he wouldn't be a springbok. Why does he have those springy legs? What would he do with them?'

'Right,' said the young lady very softly.

'So all of the animals together make the jungle what it is. And every one of them needs what it is. When there's a Water Truce, each one stops hunting or being hunted to preserve the jungle for all.'

Her features were still indiscernible due to the distance between us. All we could see of her was a rounded figure with long straight black hair falling to the sides of her head. But now we saw her nod a short nod of understanding. We all stood or sat where we were without the faintest notion of what should be done next. But then something marvellous occurred. Walter sang out in a powerful voice to her.

'Now Young Sissie, let me tell you something from myself. I don't know you and you don't know me, but it doesn't matter. We've reached the Water Truce with you. That's for sure.'

'Water Truce with *me*?' said the girl.

'Yes, my Sissie. We don't care to go on if you are going to opt out of this game. Not one of us are going on with today if you opt out – not with today and not with tomorrow. John!' he called out to me. 'Get me a loudspeaker!'

I heard and promptly sped down the flights of steps and breathlessly begged the security guard for a loudspeaker. He handed me one within seconds and I began my climb back up to the roof. It was placed in Walter's hand within four minutes of his request. Now Walter walked straight ahead of himself to the edge of the roof where he stopped a metre away. The girl sat twelve metres to his right near the corner of the rectangle upon which we stood. Walter could see more detail of her now: her very pale skin and sincere expression. She was intent upon him. Walter then pressed down the red button of the loudspeaker and drew it to his lips. These words rang out across University Boulevard where the students were commuting between lectures:

'Hear me! Hear me please! Stop where you are, every one of you, please!'

I hurried to the area on Walter's left-hand side to look over to the Boulevard. There were thirty to forty students who had in fact stopped walking and were standing, staring up to Walter. Others arrived even as I watched and followed the example of their peers.

'Thank you for stopping, because there is something vitally important I need to announce to you all. From this moment forth there will be a Water Truce. Let it be said and known as clearly as can be. From now on, things are not going on in the same way. Everything is different, because there is a Water Truce. A Water Truce means that we are not going on with our daily work today.'

The device was projecting Walter's voice resoundingly, so that the moment was invested with a drama of awesome proportions.

'Nor will we go on with our daily work tomorrow. And so it will be forever – until: this Young Sissie agrees to come down back to the ground. You all know she is here. She is your sister. And we don't want the new days to come to us if it will be without her.' He turned to face the girl and spoke to her now, but he had deactivated the loudspeaker.

'Sissie, our hopes are bound up in you. Do you understand? To us, all the sky and all the clouds and all our dreams mean nothing if you opt out. We only want to keep walking and dreaming and hoping if you are here with us.'

Then Walter pressed down on the button once again and addressed the crowd, which had swelled to double or triple what it had been.

'We're going to kneel down now, to show we're not going to go on.' And with this Walter kneeled down. I could see the crowds of students, workers and staff members clearly from my vantage-point, and what I saw presently was this: every solitary one of them proceeded to kneel down onto the ground. The girl was watching all this and could safely be described as astonished. I kneeled. She looked at me, and then gazed behind me to see Brian kneeling. She was silent. I only saw, in this loud, bellowing silence, a tear hang on to her cheek before dropping to the brick surface, then another tear which had made its way to her chin also drop down. She sobbed and I saw her petite body shudder. Then arrived on the roof the young lady's father, a small sweet-faced man of late middle age. He hesitated and when she saw him her figure perked up, and as she rose to meet him he rushed to her. They met in a glorious hug that made mincemeat of my insides. The crowds of students who were missing the start of their biology and actuarial science lectures had not seen a better day than this one. They exploded in great cheers. I and Brian felt every one of our muscles melt into the ground under our knees.

CHAPTER SIX

The Saturday evening was humid and pregnant with potential and there was an invigorating trepidation in my heart. The turnout at the Council Theatre was pleasing and the late arrivals kept on appearing. Staff members were there, socialising in the lobby with glasses of white wine. Most of the audience was going to be students and something about this year made them a very lively bunch, the kind who called out and whooped in performances. Even now as they filed into the hall leisurely from the lobby their laughter was raucous. This seemed to offer something promising for me yet would always also pose a threat. Would my performers be able to withstand an unexpected reaction from the crowd? I must admit I did feel, in any case, the fatherly pride in myself even now before anything had been proven, because I had in fact met the day through the months of varied stresses and diversions. Now there was the luxury of plush grey carpets, polite and well-dressed refreshment vendors and the dramatically high ceilings of the Council Theatre. I wandered in these minutes back and forth between the lobby and the hall, seeking something to correct and save at the last hour, but all I met with was congratulations and the easy spirit of a blessed night.

Finally, I saw her. My heart swelled and glowed luminously within me. She was standing in pause just within the revolving door, looking around the room a little warily. But her face was made up carefully and over her shoulders hung a turquoise shawl. What a strange experience to fall in love with a woman on behalf of another man! I did not approach her but only waited and her eyes settled on me. I stepped towards her twice.

'Good evening Jane,' I said.

'Good evening John,' said she.

'I am so very glad you came,' I said.

She was latching her purse for the moment and, overcoming some small struggle within her, said, 'So am I,' and she looked up with the smile of a living spirit.

'I'll show you to your seat,' I said. 'I've saved you the best one.'

She nodded gracefully and made the first step. I led her to the front row, the fourth seat from the left. She did not feel the need to make conversation or gaze around in search of an acquaintance. She only skimmed through the programme briefly and looked up to the stage in dignified expectation. The dissonance between her hard-won dignity and the latent raucousness in the student body gave me cause for some worry. Everyone had filed in and the doors were shut.

The lights in all corners were extinguished and an unexpected pitch darkness fell. The students whooped and whistled. But almost immediately a soft yellow light grew from the right and left endpoints of the stage, and our view centralised on the silhouette of a single man standing mid-stage. More whooping followed and my heart fluttered about. Then, however, stronger white light flourished around us and the features of Walter became apparent. Applause followed. Seated on a high stool, he straightened his bent neck and appraised the audience with confidence. Then his voice filled the room and warmed my heart with pride, because was it not due to me that this particular striking voice was gracing this hall, even now?

'The white man,' called Walter, 'has a worried mind.'

'Yeah! So worried!' a young man in the audience shouted out. Walter's aplomb, though, lacked nothing and commanded back the room's decorum.

'He walks around worried day and night. Take for example my boss: he worries even at the end of the day when the work has been done. But let me tell you all: I too feel the weight of a heavy idea on my head each morning. I admit it: I am like the white man. I am a worrier.

'And do you want to know what this worry is, that returns to me each morning, and spoils my morning coffee? I'll tell you. As I'm fastening my shoes, I catch a glimpse of my reflection in the glass of an old picture in my lounge. It's only through the side of my eye that I see the reflection and only for a moment. But I'm scared to look directly at that glass because the idea has already got me worried.

'The idea is that the dumb walls of my house are watching me become nothing, year after year. That I *am* just a figure that moves and takes up space and flickers past the mirror twice a day. That I could never be known in the way one friend knows another friend, only in the way you know this pane of glass or that knife and fork.

'I am a fisherman. Therefore, the most important thing is that I manage to trudge over the old brown nets to the boat on time, but first over the pavement past the fish-and-chips patrons without offending them too much by the smell of my clothes and the tears in my overalls. Also, I should watch my manners as I go.

'So I trudge with a smile and a quicker clip to my step, so you might see yet again, for the twenty-sixth consecutive time, a burnished smile on my face as I go on my way: a fisherman's smile. Then you might be pleased by the impression of predictable consistency I offer. And, though you will never call to me, never know my name and never be moved to offer me a ten-rand note, at least when you pay your bill and search for the keys to your car, you might accept in your heart that God made me just as he made the pebbles of the beach. Because after all, both of us are *consistently* unthreatening, are we not?'

The crowd loved this and stirred all the while with affirmations and amens. Walter was their shepherd and they searched for the smallest hint of his will. I was sitting in the second row and checked on Mrs Sabukwana throughout. She was an unmoving rather plump-looking figure in the dark who sat slightly open-mouthed.

'And there's something else,' continues Walter, 'another idea – that haunts my days, and though it haunts them secretly I'll tell you about it openly. The idea is that there's a room full of food made precisely according to my taste and pots of sweet tea and where I might feel *just* the way I like to. But I'll never break into this room; I'll never know where it is. There's a person, a man, I might know and with whom a brotherly love might be kindled. And I might be able to comfort this man in a time of need. But I will never meet this man because I must be standing at the docks at 5:15 am, ready and waiting, and at the end of the day I have to go home to unwind, and why would I stop anywhere unusual on the way home?

'I must admit that during the day there is enough luminescence in things to console my heart. Every sight my eyes see is full of an otherworldly glow, so that even as I purchase a loaf of bread at the café, my heart feels the promise of a thousand days of bliss. But invisible in the air, wherever I go, is this thought lingering and waiting. And when night has come, I see it. It is a vision of waste: of footsteps made to my broken-down cottage when they could have been made to a certain other house I can't quite see in my head. Waste of eyes I use to look up at the stars on my way home at night, when I remember I have forgotten to watch them for weeks on end and probably will forget for several weeks more. And I know there is another man who surveys them lovingly and caresses the twinkling of each one with his eyes all through the night. And most of all: waste of me myself when only the four poor walls of my house know me, and no other set of four walls, and no other men but the fifteen men I meet on my daily rounds. I see a vision of myself doing only what I do and nothing else. It's in the tricky few minutes when I take off my boots, before I put on the radio. Then it is that the darkness inserts that thought into my head. And, just in the last half-minute as I'm walking to the radio to turn it on, it asks a cruel question in my ear: is it just an inane song you are singing to the night, Walter Sabukwana? And then when I find a station that I like, and I'm starting to warm up and I'm beginning to sip my beer, then that evil voice speaks again in my ear. You know what it says? It says: Walter, though you look forward and hope, and keep rekindling the looking forward and the hope, at evening time the night closes in regardless. The day's hours will cease in any case.'

Walter stepped back from his microphone with a motion of finality. The masculine voices in the audience broke out in throaty praise and most men stood up, some upon their seats. Mrs Sabukwana clapped effeminately and in silhouette her expression looked sincere and awe-struck. The lights had dimmed and Walter had disappeared from stage but the applause continued for some time.

It was after the entire performance, when my students had done impressively in their own right, due to tens of sessions during which they had watched and imitated Walter under my dogged direction, that Walter and Jane met for the first time in months. They walked towards each other across the grey-carpeted lobby, and stopped each before the other at a respectful space. At first they were silent and only watched each other's eyes.

'Walter,' Jane said, 'I had no idea you were so . . . wonderful.'

Walter had changed back into his black jeans, white T-shirt and leather jacket. He was abashed.

'Hello Jane,' he said. 'You look like a queen.'

From a mature face that certainly did not think of itself as beautiful, a blush now flashed.

'No, I don't,' she said.

'You really really do,' said Walter. 'You are definitely the loveliest lady here tonight.'

The blush that threatened to come from this was too much, so she waved away his word and looked down to the ground.

'I mean it,' he said. 'All the young girls, their beauty is like the beauty of a puppy. Your beauty is the beauty of a human being.' She consented to gaze at him as he went on.

My place was elsewhere at that point so I left, but now you know some of the true-life story of True-life Walter, the famous performance-poet.

CHAPTER SEVEN

The last part of the story to tell, I suppose, is the story of my own turnaround. I gave up my office, my career; I gave up Johannesburg. It takes less time than you might think to accustom yourself to the life of a fisherman. This is not to say there is no bookshelf in my cottage, because there is, where I keep the few volumes I brought along with me. And when Paul and Sallie see them, they ask, don't I miss my career? I tell them, what is better: to read about a dance, or to dance?

I don't keep up contacts very much, because I know they all would ask: How did it happen? There isn't really any way to explain. It has something to do with Louis Botha Road when the early evening breathes its first cool breath and people collect at the taxi stops. It has a lot to do with the waves on Hout Bay Beach and the rusty boats. It even has to do with speeding on a motorbike over a deserted street without a helmet at midnight. I never denied my mind was fickle and I was easily mesmerised. Neither did I deny that I am too extreme by nature and prone to make impetuous decisions. My nature, then, got the better of me. These are words you may be able to understand – words from your own mouth. Let me tell you the last words, though, from *my* mouth. On cold winter nights, here in the village, we get together for fish and potato braais. Sallie brings the box wine. I bring out my pipe and offer the boys a smoke. And the taste of freshly braaid fish – Ay! There's nothing like it my brother.